THE BLACK MONK

AND

PEASANTS

To Fred
eat well, get rest, laugh
Bruce

ANTON CHEKHOV

THE BLACK MONK

AND

PEASANTS

Translated by Ronald Wilks

penguin books

PENGUIN BOOKS
Published by the Penguin Group
Penguin Books USA Inc., 375 Hudson Street,
New York, New York 10014, U.S.A.
Penguin Books Ltd, 27 Wrights Lane, London W8 5TZ, England
Penguin Books Australia Ltd, Ringwood, Victoria, Australia
Penguin Books Canada Ltd, 10 Alcorn Avenue,
Toronto, Ontario, Canada M4V 3B2
Penguin Books (N.Z.) Ltd, 182–190 Wairau Road,
Auckland 10, New Zealand

Penguin Books Ltd, Registered Offices:
Harmondsworth, Middlesex, England

"The Black Monk" is taken from *The Duel and Other Stories* and
"Peasants" from *The Kiss and Other Stories*, published by Penguin Books.
This edition published 1995.

Translation copyright © Ronald Wilks, 1982, 1984.
All rights reserved

ISBN 0 14 60.0036 6

Printed in the United States of America

Except in the United States of America, this book is sold subject to the
condition that it shall not, by way of trade or otherwise, be lent, re-sold,
hired out, or otherwise circulated without the publisher's prior consent
in any form of binding or cover other than that in which it is published
and without a similar condition including this condition being imposed
on the subsequent purchaser.

CONTENTS

The Black Monk

I

Andrey Kovrin, MA, was exhausted, his nerves were shattered. He did not take any medical treatment but mentioned his condition in passing to a doctor friend over a bottle of wine, and was advised to spend the spring and summer in the country. And as it happened he received just then a long letter from Tanya Pesotskaya, inviting him to come and stay at Borisovka. So he decided he really must get away.

At first – this was in April – he went to his own estate Kovrinka, where he lived on his own for three weeks. Then after waiting until the roads were passable, he drove off in a carriage to see his former guardian and mentor Pesotsky the horticulturalist, who was famous throughout Russia. It was no more than about fifty miles from Kovrinka to Pesotsky's place at Borisovka and it was pure joy travelling along the soft road in spring, in a comfortable sprung carriage.

Pesotsky's house was huge, with columns, peeling plaster lions, and a footman in coat and tails at the entrance. The gloomy, severe, old-fashioned park was strictly laid out in English style, stretched almost half a mile from the house to the river, and ended in a precipitous clayey bank where pines grew, their exposed roots resembling shaggy paws. Down below, the water glinted uninvitingly, sandpipers flew past squeaking plaintively, and it was generally the kind of place to make you want to sit down and write a ballad. But near the house itself, in the courtyard and the orchard, which took up about eighty acres, including the nursery beds, it was cheerful and lively, even in bad weather. Nowhere, except at Pesotsky's, had Kovrin seen such wonderful roses, lilies, camellias, so many different tulips, with colours ranging from white to soot-black, such a profusion of flowers. It was only the beginning of spring and the real splendours of the flowerbeds were still hidden in the hothouses. But the flowers in bloom along the paths – and here and there in the beds – were enough to make you feel that you were in the very kingdom of tender hues as you strolled in the garden, especially early in the morning, when dew sparkled on every petal.

The ornamental section of the garden, which Pesotsky disparagingly called 'sheer nonsense', had seemed like a fairyland to Kovrin as a child. The oddities, elaborate monstrosities and travesties of nature that were to be seen here! There were trellised fruit-trees, a pear-tree shaped like a Lombardy poplar, globe-shaped oaks and limes, an apple-tree umbrella, arches, initials, candelabra, and even an '1862' made from plums – this was the year Pesotsky first took up horticulture. Here also were fine, graceful saplings with straight, firm stems like palm-trees, and only after a very close look could you tell that they were gooseberries or blackcurrants. But what most of all made the garden a cheerful, lively place was the constant activity. From dawn to dusk gardeners with wheelbarrows, hoes and watering-cans swarmed like ants near the trees and bushes, on the paths and flowerbeds.

Kovrin arrived at the Pesotskys' after nine in the evening.

He found Tanya and her father Yegor in a terribly worried state. The clear, starry sky and the thermometer foretold frost towards morning, but the head gardener Ivan Karlych had gone off to town and there was no one left they could rely on.

During supper, they talked only of this morning frost and decided that Tanya would not go to bed, but would go round the orchard after midnight to check if everything was all right, while Yegor would get up at three, even earlier perhaps. Kovrin sat with Tanya the whole evening and after midnight went with her into the garden. It was cold and there was a strong smell of burning. In the big orchard, called 'commercial' as it brought Yegor Pesotsky several thousand roubles profit every year, a dense, black, acrid smoke was spreading over the ground and enveloping the trees, saving all those thousands from the frost. Here the trees were planted like draughts pieces, in straight, even rows, like columns of soldiers. This strict, pedantic regularity, plus the fact that all the trees were exactly the same height, all of them having absolutely identical crowns and trunks, made a monotonous, even boring picture. Kovrin and Tanya walked between the rows, where bonfires of manure, straw and all kind of refuse were smouldering, and every now and then they met workers drifting through the smoke like shadows. Only cherries, plums and certain varieties of apple were in bloom, but the whole orchard was drowning in smoke. Kovrin breathed a deep breath only when they reached the nurseries.

'When I was a child the smoke used to make me sneeze,' he said, shrugging his shoulders, 'but I still don't understand why this smoke saves the plants from frost.'

3

'Smoke is a substitute for clouds when the sky is clear . . .'
Tanya said.

'But what use are *they*?'

'You don't normally get a frost when it's dull and overcast.'

'That's right!'

He laughed and took her arm. Her broad, very serious face, chill from the cold, with its fine black eyebrows, the raised coat collar which cramped her movements, her whole slim, graceful body, her dress tucked up from the dew – all this moved him deeply.

'Heavens, how you've grown up!' he said. 'Last time I left here, five years ago, you were still a child. You were so thin, long-legged, bareheaded, with that short little dress you used to wear. And I teased you and called you a heron . . . How time changes everything!'

'Yes, five years!' Tanya sighed. 'A lot of water has flowed under the bridge since then. Tell me, Andrey, in all honesty,' she said in an animated voice, peering into his face, 'have you grown tired of us? But why am I asking you this? You're a man, you live your own interesting life, you're an eminent person . . . Becoming like strangers to each other is really so natural! Anyway, Andrey, I want you to treat us as your family, we have a right to that.'

'But I do, Tanya.'

'Word of honour?'

'Yes, word of honour.'

'You were surprised before that we had so many of your photos. You must know Father idolizes you. At times I think he loves you more than me. He's proud of you. You are a scholar, a remarkable person, you've made a dazzling career for yourself and he's convinced this is because he brought you up. I let him think this, I don't see why I should stop him.'

Dawn was breaking – this was particularly evident from the clarity with which puffs of smoke and the tree tops were outlined now in the air. Nightingales were singing and the cries of quails came from the fields.

'But it's time for bed,' Tanya said. 'Besides that, it's cold.' She took his arm. 'Thanks for coming, Andrey. Our friends aren't very interesting, not that we have many. All we have is the garden, garden, garden, nothing else.' She laughed. 'First-class, second-class, Oporto, rennets and winter apples, budding, grafting. Our whole life has gone into this garden, I dream of nothing but apple- and pear-trees. Of course, it's all very nice and useful, but sometimes I want something else, to break the monotony. I remember the times you came for the holidays, or just for a short visit, how the house became somehow fresher and brighter then, as though the covers had been taken off the chandeliers and furniture. I was a little girl then, but I did understand.'

She spoke for a long time and with great feeling. Suddenly Kovrin was struck by the idea that he might even conceive an affection for this small, fragile, loquacious creature during the course of the summer, become attracted to her and fall in love. In their situation that would be so natural and possible! He was both touched and amused by the thought. He leant down towards that dear, worried face and softly sang:

'Onegin, I will not hide it,
I love Tatyana madly . . .'

Yegor Pesotsky was up already when they returned to the house. Kovrin did not feel like sleeping, got into conversation with the old man and went back to the garden with him. Yegor Pesotsky was a tall, broad-shouldered man, with a large paunch. Although he suffered from short breath, he always walked so fast it was hard keeping up with him. He had an extremely worried look and was always hurrying off somewhere as if all would be lost should he be just one minute late.

'It's a peculiar thing, my dear boy,' he began, then paused for breath. 'As you see, it's freezing down on the ground, but just you hold a thermometer on a stick about twelve feet above it and you'll find it's warm there . . . Why is it?'

'I honestly don't know,' Kovrin said, laughing.

'Hm . . . one can't know everything of course . . . However capacious your brain is, it won't accommodate everything, Philosophy's more your line, isn't it?'

'I give lectures on psychology, but my main interest is philosophy.'

'And you're not bored?'

'On the contrary, it's my life.'

'Well, God bless you . . .' Yegor Pesotsky murmured, thoughtfully stroking his grey side-whiskers. 'God bless you . . . I'm very pleased for you . . . very pleased, dear boy.'

But suddenly he pricked up his ears, pulled a horrified face, ran to one side and soon disappeared in the clouds of smoke behind the trees.

'Who tied a horse to that apple-tree?' the despairing, heart-rending cry rang out. 'What swine, what scum dared to tie a horse to an apple-tree? Good Lord! They've ruined, frozen, polluted, mucked everything up! The garden's ruined! Ruined! Oh, God!'

He went back to Kovrin, looking exhausted, outraged. 'What can you do with this confounded riff-raff?' he said tearfully, flinging his arms out helplessly. 'Last night Stepka was carting manure and tied his horse to the apple-tree. He twisted the reins so hellishly tight, damn him, that the bark's rubbed off. How could he do it? I had words with him, but the idiot just stood gaping. Hanging's too good for him!'

After he had calmed down he put his arms round Kovrin and kissed him on the cheek. 'Well, God bless, God bless . . .' he muttered. 'I'm very pleased you came. I can't say how glad I am . . . Thanks.'

Then, at the same rapid pace and with that same worried look, he toured the whole garden, showing his former ward all the conservatories, greenhouses, cold frames, and the two apiaries he called the 'wonder of the century'.

As they walked along, the sun rose, filling the garden with a bright light. It grew warm. Anticipating a fine, cheerful, long day, Kovrin recalled that in fact it was only the beginning of May and that the whole summer lay ahead – just as bright, cheerful and long, and suddenly there welled up within him that feeling of radiant, joyous youth he had known in his childhood, when he had run around this garden. And he embraced the old man in turn and kissed him tenderly. Both of them, deeply moved, went into the house and drank tea 7 from old-fashioned porcelain cups, with cream and rich pastries. These little things again reminded Kovrin of his childhood and youth. The beautiful present, the freshly awakened impressions of the past, blended together: they had a somewhat inhibiting effect, but none the less gave him a feeling of well-being.

He waited for Tanya to wake up, drank coffee with her, went for a stroll, and then returned to his room and sat down to work. He read attentively, took notes, now and again looking up at the open window or the fresh flowers that stood, still moist with dew, in vases on the table, then lowering his eyes on his book again; it seemed every vein in his body was pulsating and throbbing with pleasure.

2

In the country he continued to lead the same nervous, restless life as in town. He read and wrote a great deal, studied Italian, and on his strolls took pleasure in the thought that he would soon be back at work again. Everyone was amazed he slept so little. If he chanced to doze off during the day for half an hour, he could not sleep at all later and would emerge from a night of insomnia vigorous and cheerful, as if nothing was wrong.

He talked a lot, drank wine and smoked expensive cigars. Young ladies who lived nearby called on the Pesotskys almost every day and played the piano and sang with Tanya. Sometimes a young gentleman from the neighbourhood, an excellent violinist, would call. Kovrin would listen so hungrily to the playing and singing it tired him out, and the exhaustion was plainly visible from the way his eyelids seemed to stick together and his head dropped to one side.

One evening, after tea, he was sitting on the balcony reading. At the same time Tanya, who sang soprano, together with one of the young ladies – a contralto – and the young violinist, were practising Brag's famous *Serenade*. Kovrin listened hard to the words (they were Russian) but could not understand them at all. Finally, after putting his book aside and listening very closely, he did understand: a young girl, with a morbid imagination, was in her garden one night and heard some mysterious sounds, so beautiful and strange, she had to admit that their harmony was something divine, incomprehensible to mere mortals as it soared up again into the heavens whence it came. Kovrin began to feel sleepy. He rose to his feet, wearily walked up and down the drawing-room, then the ballroom. When the singing stopped, he took Tanya by the arm and went out onto the balcony with her.

'Since early this morning I haven't been able to get a certain legend out of my mind,' he said. 'I can't remember if I read it somewhere or if I heard it, but it's really quite strange – doesn't appear to make any sense at all. I should say from the start that it's not distinguished for its clarity. A thousand years ago a certain monk, dressed in black, was walking across a desert – somewhere in Syria or Arabia . . . A few miles from where he was walking a fisherman saw another black monk slowly moving across the surface of a lake. This second monk was a mirage. Now forget the laws of 9 optics, which the legend apparently doesn't acknowledge and listen to what happened next. The mirage produced another one. This second mirage produced a third, so that the image of the black monk began to be transmitted endlessly from one layer of the atmosphere to the other. He was sighted in Africa, then Spain, India, the far North ... He finally left the earth's atmosphere and now wanders through the whole universe, never meeting the conditions which would make it possible for him to fade away. Perhaps he'll be seen somewhere on Mars now, or on some star in the Southern Cross. But, my dear, the essence, the real crux of the legend is this: precisely one thousand years after that monk first walked across the desert, the mirage will return to the earth's atmosphere and appear to people. And it seems these thousand years are almost up. According to the legend, we can expect the black monk any day now.'

'A strange mirage,' said Tanya, who did not care for the legend.

'But the most amazing thing is,' Kovrin said, laughing, 'I just can't remember what prompted me to think of it. Did I read it somewhere? Did I hear about it? Perhaps the black monk was only a dream? I swear to God, I can't remember. But I'm intrigued by this legend. I've been thinking about it all day.'

Leaving Tanya to her guests, he went out of the house and strolled by the flowerbeds, deep in thought. The sun was setting. The freshly watered flowers gave off a moist, irritating scent. In the house the singing had started again; from the distance the violin sounded like a human voice. Kovrin racked his brains trying to remember where he had read or heard about that legend as he walked unhurriedly towards the park, reaching the river before he knew where he was.

He descended the path that ran down a steep bank, past bare roots, to the water, where he disturbed some sandpipers and frightened two ducks away. Here and there on the gloomy pines gleamed the last rays of the setting sun, but evening had already come over the surface of the river. Kovrin crossed the foot-bridge to the other side. Before him lay a broad field full of young rye not yet in ear. There was no human habitation, not a living soul out there, and it seemed the path would lead him to that same unknown, mysterious spot where the sun had just set and where the evening glow spread its flames so magnificently over all that wide expanse.

'So much space, freedom, peace here!' Kovrin thought as he walked along the path. 'The whole world seems to be looking at me, has gone silent, and is waiting for me to understand it.'

But just then some ripples spread across the rye and a gentle evening breeze lightly caressed his bare head. A moment later there was another gust, stronger this time, and the rye rustled and he could hear the dull murmur of the pines behind him. Kovrin stood motionless in astonishment. On the horizon a tall black column was rising up into the sky, like a whirlwind or tornado. Its outlines were blurred, but he could see at once that it was not standing still, but moving at terrifying speed straight towards him – and the nearer it came, the smaller and clearer it grew. Kovrin leapt aside into the rye to make way – and he was only just in time ... A monk in black vestments, grey-haired and with black eyebrows, his arms across his chest, flashed past; his bare feet did not touch the ground. After he had raced on another six yards he looked round at Kovrin, nodded and gave him a friendly, but artful, smile. What a pale, terribly pale, thin face though! Growing larger again, he flew across the river, struck the clayey bank and the pines without making a sound, passed straight through and disappeared into thin air.

'So, there it is ...' murmured Kovrin. 'That shows there's truth in the legend.'

Without trying to find an explanation for this strange apparition and satisfied that he had managed to get such a close look, not only at the black vestments, but even at the monk's face and eyes, he went back to the house feeling pleasantly excited.

People were strolling peacefully in the park and garden, the musicians were playing in the house, so only he had seen the monk. He had a strong urge to tell Tanya and Yegor Pesotsky about everything, but he realized they would surely think the story crazy and be scared stiff. Better keep quiet about it. He laughed out loud, sang, danced a mazurka; he was in high spirits and everyone – Tanya, her guests – found that he really had a radiant, inspired look about him that evening, that he was most interesting.

After supper, when the guests had left, he went to his room and lay on the couch. He wanted to think about the monk, but a moment later, in came Tanya.

'Here, Andrey, read Father's articles,' she said, handing him a bundle of pamphlets and offprints. 'They're wonderful, he's an excellent writer.'

'I wouldn't say that!' Yegor Pesotsky said, forcing a laugh as he followed her into the room; he felt embarrassed. 'Don't listen to her, please! Don't read them! But if you need something to make you sleep, then go ahead. They're an excellent soporific!'

'In my opinion they're magnificent,' Tanya said with great conviction. 'Read them, Andrey, and persuade Father to write more often. He could write a whole course in horticulture.'

Yegor Pesotsky gave a forced laugh, blushed and started speaking in the way shy authors usually do. In the end he gave in. 'In that case, read Gaucher's article first, then these short ones in Russian,' he muttered, turning over the pamphlets with trembling hands. 'Otherwise you won't understand a thing. Before you read my objections, you must know what it is I'm objecting to. However, it's rubbish . . . boring. What's more, I think it's time for bed.'

Tanya went out. Yegor Pesotsky sat beside Kovrin on the couch and sighed deeply. 'Yes, my dear boy,' he began after a short silence. 'Yes, my dear Master of Arts. Here I am

writing articles and exhibiting at shows and winning medals
. . . They say Pesotsky has "apples as big as your head" and
that he made his fortune with his orchard. Pesotsky is
monarch of all he surveys, in short. But, you may ask, what's
the point of it all? The garden is really beautiful, a show-
garden in fact. It's not so much a garden as a complete
institution, of the greatest importance to the State, a step, so
to speak, towards a new era in Russian economics and
industry. But what's the point of it? What's the use?'

'It speaks for itself.'

'That's not what I mean. I'd like to know, what will
happen to the garden when I die? It won't be kept up to its
present standard for more than one month. The secret of my
success isn't that it's a big garden, with lots of gardeners, but
because I love the work – do you follow? Perhaps I love it
better than myself. I work from dawn till dusk. The grafting,
pruning, planting – I do them all myself. When people start
helping me, I get jealous and irritated until I'm downright
rude to them. The whole secret is *love*, and by that I mean
the keen eye and head of the master looking after his own
place, the feeling that comes over you when you've gone
visiting for an hour and you just sit still. But your heart's not
there, you're miles away – afraid something might be going
wrong in the garden. And when I die who'll look after it?
Who'll do the work? The head gardener? The ordinary
gardeners? What do you think? So let me tell you, dear boy,
the principal enemy in our work isn't hares, cockchafers or
frost, but the man who doesn't care.'

'And Tanya?' laughed Kovrin. 'She couldn't possibly do

more harm than a hare. She loves the work, she understands it.'

'Yes, she loves and understands it. If the garden passes into *her* hands after my death and she takes charge, I could hope for nothing better. But supposing she marries, God forbid?' Yegor Pesotsky whispered and gave Kovrin a frightened look. 'This is my point! She'll marry, have children and then she'll have no time to think about the garden. But my main worry is her marrying some young whipper-snapper who'll grow greedy, rent the garden out to some market-woman and it'll all go to rack and ruin within a year! In this kind of business women are like the plague!'

Pesotsky sighed and was silent for a few minutes. 'Perhaps it's just egotism, but I'm telling you quite frankly: I don't want Tanya to marry. I'm afraid! There's that young fop who comes here scraping his fiddle. I know Tanya won't marry him, I know that very well, but I just can't stand the sight of him. On the whole I'm quite a crank, dear boy. I admit it.' Pesotsky got up and paced the room excitedly; it was plain he wanted to say something very important, but he couldn't bring himself to.

'I'm extremely fond of you and I'll be open with you,' he said at last, stuffing his hands into his pockets. 'I'm usually quite straightforward when it comes to certain ticklish questions and I'm telling you exactly what I think – I can't stand these so-called "innermost thoughts". I'm telling you straight: you're the only man I wouldn't mind marrying my daughter. You're clever, you have feelings and you wouldn't let my beloved work perish. But the main reason is – I love you like a son . . . and I'm proud of you. If Tanya and yourself became fond of each other, well then, I'd be very glad, happy even. I'm telling you straight, without frills, as an honest man.'

Kovrin burst out laughing. Pesotsky opened the door to go out and stopped on the threshold. 'If Tanya gave you a son I'd make a gardener out of him,' he said thoughtfully. 'However, that's an idle dream . . . Good night.'

Left alone, Kovrin settled himself more comfortably on the couch and started on the articles. One bore the title *Intermedial Cultivation*, another *A few Observations on Mr Z's Remarks on Double-trenching in New Gardens*, and another *More about Grafting Dormant Buds*; and there were other titles like that. But what a restless, uneven tone, what highly charged, almost pathological fervour! Here was an article with apparently the most inoffensive title and unexceptionable subject – the winter dessert apple. But Pesotsky first weighed in with an *audiatur altera pars** and ended with *sapienti sat†*, interpolating these dicta with a whole torrent of venomous animadversions apropos the 'learned ignorance of our self-appointed gentlemen-horticulturalists who look down on nature from their Olympian heights'; or Gaucher, 'whose reputation was made by ignoramuses and dilettantes'. These remarks were followed by the totally irrelevant, forced, sham regret for the fact that it was no longer legal to birch peasants who stole fruit and damaged trees in the process.

'It's a fine, pleasant, healthy occupation, but even here it's passion and warfare,' Kovrin thought. 'Probably, it's because

---

* 'Let the other side be heard.'

† 'Enough for a wise man.'

intellectuals are neurotic and over-sensitive everywhere, in all walks of life. Perhaps it can't be avoided.'

He thought of Tanya who liked Pesotsky's articles so much. She was not tall, was pale and thin, with protruding collarbones; her dark, clever, staring eyes were always peering, seeking something. She walked just like her father, taking short, quick steps. Very talkative, she loved to argue and would accompany the most trivial phrase with highly expressive mimicry and gesticulations. She was probably highly strung.

Kovrin read on, but he understood nothing and gave up. That same, agreeable feeling of excitement he had had when dancing his mazurka and listening to the music made him weary now and stirred a multitude of thoughts. He stood up and started walking round the room, thinking about the black monk. It occurred to him that if he alone had seen that strange, supernatural apparition, then he must be ill and a prey to hallucinations. This thought frightened him, but not for long.

'In fact I feel fine. I'm not harming anyone. So that means there's nothing bad in these hallucinations,' he thought and felt fine again.

He sat on the couch and clasped his head to hold in check that incomprehensible feeling of joy which filled his whole being; then he paced up and down again and started to work. But the ideas he found in the book left him unsatisfied. He wanted something gigantic, immense, staggering. Towards dawn he undressed and reluctantly got into bed. After all, he had to sleep!

When he heard Pesotsky's footsteps receding into the garden, Kovrin rang the bell and told the servant to bring him some wine. After enjoying a few glasses of claret his senses grew dim and he fell asleep.

4

Pesotsky and Tanya had frequent quarrels and said nasty things to each other. One morning, after a squabble about something, Tanya burst into tears and went to her room. She didn't appear for lunch, or tea. At first Pesotsky walked around solemnly and pompously, as if he wanted to make it known that he considered justice and order more important than anything else in the world. But he could not keep up the pose for long and lost heart. Sadly he wandered through the park, sighing the whole time, 'Ah, Good Lord, Good Lord!' and he did not eat a thing for dinner. Finally, full of guilt and remorse, he knocked on the locked door and called out timidly, 'Tanya! Tanya?'

A weak voice, drained by tears, but still determined, replied from behind the door, 'Leave me alone, I beg you.'

The anguish of the master and mistress was reflected all over the house, even in the gardeners. Kovrin was immersed in his interesting work, but in the end he too felt bored and embarrassed. Trying to dispel the prevailing unpleasant atmosphere, he decided to intervene and towards evening knocked at Tanya's door. She let him in.

'Come now, you should be ashamed!' he joked, looking in amazement at Tanya's tear-stained, mournful face that was covered in red blotches. 'Surely it's not as bad as all that? Now, now!'

'If you only knew how he torments me!' she said and copious, bitter tears welled from her large eyes. 'He's tormented the life out of me,' she went on, wringing her hands. 'I didn't say *anything* to him . . . nothing at all. I only said we don't need to keep on extra workers when . . . when we can engage day-labourers if we want to. You know, our gardeners have been standing idle for a whole week. That's all I said, but he shouted and said many insulting, deeply offensive things. Why?'

'Now, that's enough, enough,' Kovrin said, smoothing her hair. 'You've had your quarrel and a good cry, and that's enough. You must stop being angry now, it's not good . . . especially as he loves you so very much.'

'He's ruined my whole life,' Tanya continued, sobbing. 'All I hear is insults and abuse . . . He thinks there's no place for me in this house. Agreed. He's right. I'll leave this place tomorrow, get a job as a telegraphist . . . That's what I'll do.'

'Come now, there's no need to cry, Tanya. Please don't, my dear . . . You're both quick-tempered, easily upset, and you're both to blame. Come on, I'll make peace between you.'

Kovrin spoke with feeling, convincingly, but she kept on crying, her shoulders twitching and her hands clenched as if something really terrible had happened to her. He felt all the more sorry for her because, although her grief was nothing serious, she was suffering deeply. How little it took to make this creature unhappy all day long, for her whole life perhaps! As he comforted Tanya, Kovrin thought that he wouldn't find two people who loved him so much as Tanya and her father in a month of Sundays. Having lost his father and mother as a small child, but for these two, probably, he would never have known true affection until his dying day. He would never have known that simple, disinterested love that is felt only for those who are very close, for blood relations. And he felt that this weeping, trembling girl's nerves were reacting to his own half-sick, overwrought nerves like iron to a magnet. He could never have loved a healthy, strong, rosy-cheeked woman, but that pale, weak, unhappy Tanya attracted him.

And he gladly stroked her hair and shoulders, pressed her hands and wiped away the tears ... Finally she stopped crying. For a long time she complained about her father and her hard, intolerable life in that house, imploring Kovrin to see things as she did. Then gradually, she began to smile and said sighing that God had given her *such* a bad character. In the end she laughed out loud, called herself a fool and ran out of the room.

Shortly afterwards, when Kovrin went into the garden, Pesotsky and Tanya were strolling side by side along the path as if nothing had happened. They were both eating rye bread with salt, as they were hungry.

Pleased with his success as peacemaker, Kovrin went into the park. As he sat pondering on a bench he heard the clatter of carriages and a woman's laughter – guests had arrived. As the shadows of evening fell across the garden he heard the vague sounds of a violin, voices singing, which reminded him of the black monk. Where, in what country or on what planet was that optical absurdity wandering now?

Hardly had he recalled that legend, conjuring up the dark spectre he had seen in the rye field when quite silently, without the slightest rustling, a man of medium height, his grey head uncovered, all in black, barefoot like a beggar, his black eyebrows sharply defined on his deathly white face, slipped out from behind the pine trees just opposite. Nodding his head welcomingly, this beggar or pilgrim silently came over to the bench and Kovrin could see it was the black monk. For a minute they both eyed each other – Kovrin in amazement, the monk in a friendly way, with that same rather crafty look.

'You're just a mirage,' Kovrin murmured. 'Why are you here, sitting still like that? It doesn't tally with the legend.'

'Never mind,' the monk answered softly after a brief pause, turning his face towards him. 'The legend, myself, the mirage are all products of your overheated imagination. I'm an apparition . . .'

'That means you don't exist?' Kovrin asked.

'Think what you like,' the monk said with a weak smile. 'I exist in your imagination, and your imagination is part of nature, so I exist in nature too.'

'You have a very aged, clever and extremely expressive face, as if you really have lived more than a thousand years,' Kovrin said. 'I didn't know my imagination could create such phenomena. But why are you looking at me so rapturously? Do you like me?'

'Yes. You're one of the few who are rightly called God's Chosen. You serve Eternal Truth. Your ideas, intentions, your amazing erudition, your whole life – all bear the divine, 21 heavenly stamp, since they are devoted to the Rational and the Beautiful, that is, to the Eternal.'

'You mentioned "Eternal Truth" . . . But is that within men's reach, do they need it if there's no such thing as eternal life?'

'There *is* eternal life,' the monk said.

'Do you believe in immortality?'

'Yes, of course. A great, bright future awaits you human beings. And the more men there are like you on earth, the quicker will this future come about. Without men like you serving the highest principles, living intelligently and freely, humanity would be worthless. In the normal course of events it would have to wait a long time for its life upon earth to come to an end. But you will lead it into the Kingdom of Eternal Truth a few thousand years ahead of time – this is your noble service. You are the embodiment of God's blessing which has come to dwell among men.'

'But what is the purpose of eternal life?' asked Kovrin.

'Like any other kind of life – pleasure. True pleasure is knowledge, and eternal life will afford innumerable and inexhaustible sources of knowledge: this is the meaning of the saying, "In my Father's house are many mansions."'

'If you only knew how enjoyable it is listening to you!' Kovrin said, rubbing his hands with pleasure.

'I'm very pleased.'

'But I know one thing: when you've gone I'll start worrying whether you really do exist. You're a phantom, a hallucination. Does that mean I'm mentally ill, insane?'

'Even if that were so, why let it bother you? You're ill

from overworking, you've worn yourself out. I'm trying to say that you've sacrificed your health for an idea and it won't be long before you sacrifice your very life to it. What could be better? All noble spirits blessed with gifts from on high have this as their aim.'

'If I *know* that I'm mentally ill, how can I have any faith in myself?'

'But how do you know that men of genius, in whom the whole world puts its faith, haven't seen ghosts too? Nowadays scientists say genius is akin to madness. My friend, only the mediocre, the common herd are healthy and normal. Thoughts about an age of neurosis, overwork, degeneracy and so on can seriously worry only those for whom the purpose of life lies in the present – that is, the common herd.'

'The Romans used to speak of *mens sana in corpore sano*.'

'Not all that the Greeks and Romans said is true. Heightened awareness, excitement, ecstasy – everything that distinguishes prophets, poets, martyrs to an idea, from ordinary people is hostile to man's animal side – I mean, his physical health. I repeat: if you want to be healthy and normal, go and join the herd.'

'It's strange the way you repeat things I think of myself very often,' Kovrin said. 'It's as though you spied out and eavesdropped on my most secret thoughts. But let's not talk about me. What do you mean by Eternal Truth?'

The monk did not answer. Kovrin looked at him and could not make out his face – its features had become hazy and indistinct. Then the monk's head and arms began to disappear. His torso merged with the bench and the twilight shadows, and he vanished completely.

'The hallucination's over!' Kovrin said laughing. 'A pity!'

He went back to the house happy and cheerful. The monk's few words had flattered not his pride, but his very soul, his whole being. To be one of the Chosen, to serve Eternal Truth, to stand in the ranks of those who, a thousand years ahead of time, would make men worthy of the Kingdom of God, thereby saving them from several thousand years of needless struggle, sin and suffering, to surrender, to surrender everything – youth, strength, health – to an idea, to be ready to die for the common weal – what a noble, blissful destiny! The memory of his pure, chaste, hardworking past flashed through his mind; he remembered what he had learned, what he had taught others, and he decided that the monk had not been exaggerating.

As he went through the park he met Tanya. She was wearing a different dress now.

'So you're here,' she said. 'We've all been looking for you, looking everywhere . . . But what's the matter?' she asked in surprise, studying his radiant, glowing face. 'How strange you are, Andrey.'

'I'm contented, Tanya,' Kovrin said as he put his hands on her shoulders. 'I'm more than contented, I'm happy! Tanya, dear Tanya, you're such a likeable person! Dear Tanya, I'm so glad, so glad!'

He kissed both her hands passionately and went on, 'I've just experienced some bright, wonderful, divine moments. But I can't tell you everything, because you'd call me mad or

disbelieve me. Let's talk about you. Dear, wonderful Tanya!
I love you. I'm *used* to loving you now. Having you near me,
meeting you ten times a day has become a spiritual necessity.
I don't know how I will cope when I go home.'

'Well!' Tanya laughed. 'You'll forget about us in a couple
of days. We're small fry and you're a great man.'

'No, let's be serious!' he said. 'I shall take you with me,
Tanya. Will you say yes? Will you come with me? Will you
be mine?'

'Well!' Tanya said and felt like laughing again. But she
could not and her face came out in red blotches. Her breath
came faster and she quickly went away, not towards the
house, but further into the park. 'I hadn't given it any
thought ... I hadn't thought ...' she said, wringing her
hands despairingly.

But Kovrin kept following her, still speaking with that
same radiant, rapturous expression on his face, 'I want a love
which will completely transport me, and only *you* can give
me that love, Tanya! I'm happy, so happy!'

Quite stunned, she stooped, shrank and suddenly seemed
to have aged ten years. But he found her beautiful and
shouted out in delight, 'How beautiful she is!'

5

When he heard from Kovrin that not only were they enam-
oured of each other, but that there was even going to be a
wedding, Pesotsky paced up and down for a long time, trying 25

to conceal his excitement. His hands started shaking, his neck swelled up and turned crimson. He ordered his racing drozhky to be harnessed and drove off somewhere. When Tanya saw him whipping the horses and pulling his cap almost onto his ears, she realized the kind of mood he was in, locked herself in her room and cried all day long.

The peaches and plums in the hothouses were already ripe. The packing and despatch of this delicate, temperamental cargo required a great deal of care, labour and trouble. Because of the very hot, dry summer, each tree needed watering, which involved a great deal of the gardeners' time. Swarms of caterpillars appeared, which the gardeners – even Pesotsky and Tanya – squashed with their bare fingers, much to Kovrin's disgust. Besides this, they had to take orders for fruit and trees for the autumn and conduct an extensive correspondence. And at the most critical time, when no one seemed to have a moment to spare, the harvesting started and this took half the work-force away from the garden. Extremely sunburnt, worn-out and in a dreadful mood, Pesotsky would tear off into the garden, then out into the fields, shouting that they were tearing him to pieces and that he was going to put a bullet in his head.

And now there were rows about the trousseau, to which the Pesotskys attached no little importance. The snipping of scissors, the rattle of sewing-machines, the fumes from the hot-irons, the tantrums of the dressmaker – a nervous, touchy woman – had everyone's head in a whirl in that household. And as ill luck would have it, guests turned up every day and had to be amused, fed, even put up for the night. But all this toil passed by unnoticed, as though in a mist. Tanya felt as if she had been caught quite unawares by love and happiness, although, from the age of fourteen, she had been somehow sure that Kovrin would marry her, and no one else. She was amazed, bewildered and could not believe what had happened. One moment she would feel such joy that she wanted to fly up into the clouds and offer prayers to God; another time she would suddenly remember that she would have to leave her little nest and part from her father in August; on another occasion the thought would come to her, God knows from where, that she was an insignificant, trivial sort of woman, unworthy of a great man like Kovrin, and she would go to her room, lock the door and cry bitterly for several hours. When they had visitors she would suddenly find Kovrin extremely handsome and think that all the women were in love with him and jealous of her. And her heart would fill with rapturous pride, as if she had conquered the whole world. But he only had to give some young woman a welcoming smile and she would tremble with jealousy, go to her room – and there would be tears again. These new feelings took complete hold of her, she helped her father as though she were a machine and was blind to peaches, caterpillars, workers, oblivious of how swiftly the time was passing.

Almost exactly the same thing was happening to Pesotsky. He worked from morning till night, was always hurrying off somewhere, would boil over and lose his temper, but all this in some kind of magical half-sleep. He seemed to be two different persons at once: one was the real Pesotsky, listening to the head gardener Ivan Karlych's reports of things going wrong, flaring up and clutching his head in despair; the other was not the real Pesotsky, a half-intoxicated person who would suddenly break off a conversation about business in the middle of a sentence, tap the head gardener on the shoulder and mutter, 'Whatever you say, good stock matters. His mother was an amazing, noble, brilliant woman. It was a pleasure looking at her kind, bright, pure face, the face of an angel. She was excellent at drawing, wrote poetry, spoke five languages, sang . . . The poor woman, God rest her soul, died of consumption.'

The unreal Pesotsky would continue after a brief silence, 'When he was a boy, growing up in my house, he had the same angelic, bright, kind face. And his look, his movements and his conversation were like his mother's – gentle and refined. And as for his intellect, he always staggered us with his intellect. By the way, he didn't become an MA for nothing, oh no! But you wait and see, Ivan Karlych, what he'll be like in ten years' time! There'll be no touching him!'

But at this point the real Pesotsky would suddenly take charge, pull a terrifying face, clutch his head and shout, 'The swines! They've polluted, fouled, frozen everything solid! The garden's ruined! It's finished!'

But Kovrin kept on working with his former enthusiasm and did not notice all the commotion around him. Love only added fuel to the flames. After every meeting with Tanya he would return to his room feeling happy, exultant and would pick up a book or manuscript with the same passion with which he had just kissed Tanya and declared his love. What the black monk had told him about God's Chosen, Eternal Truth, humanity's glittering future and so on lent his work a special, remarkable significance and filled his heart with pride and awareness of his own outstanding qualities. Once or twice a week he met the black monk in the park or in the house, had a talk with him, but it did not frighten him. On the contrary, it delighted him, as he was now firmly convinced that these kinds of visions visited only the select few, only outstanding men who had dedicated themselves to an idea.

One day the monk appeared at dinner time and sat by the window in the dining-room. Kovrin was overjoyed and deftly started a conversation with Pesotsky on a topic that the monk would very likely find interesting. The black visitor listened and nodded his head amiably. Pesotsky and Tanya listened too, cheerfully smiling and without suspecting that Kovrin was speaking not to them, but to his hallucination.

The Feast of the Assumption came unnoticed and soon afterwards the wedding-day, which, as Pesotsky insisted, was celebrated with 'a great splash', that is to say, with senseless festivities that went on for two whole days. They got through three thousand roubles' worth of food and drink, but with that miserable hired band, the riotous toasts and scurrying servants, the noise and the crush, they did not appreciate the expensive wines, nor the startling delicacies that had been ordered from Moscow.

6

One long winter's night Kovrin was reading a French novel in bed. Poor Tanya, who suffered from headaches in the evening as she wasn't used to town life, had long been asleep and was muttering something incoherent.

Three o'clock struck. Kovrin snuffed the candle and lay down. He remained with eyes closed for a long time, but he could not sleep, possibly because the bedroom was very hot and Tanya was talking in her sleep. At half past four he lit the candle again and this time he saw the black monk sitting in the armchair near the bed.

'Good evening,' the monk said. After a brief pause he asked, 'What are you thinking about now?'

'Fame,' Kovrin answered. 'I've just been reading a French novel about a young scholar who does stupid things and who's wasting away because of his longing for fame. This longing is something I can't understand.'

'That's because you're intelligent. You're indifferent to fame, it's a toy that doesn't interest you.'

'Yes, that's true.'

'Fame doesn't tempt you. What is flattering, or amusing, or edifying in having your name carved on a tombstone only for it to be rubbed off by time, gilding as well? Fortunately there are too many of you for humanity's weak memory to retain your names.'

'I understand that,' Kovrin agreed. 'And why should they be remembered? But let's talk about something else. Happiness, for example. What is happiness?'

When the clock struck five he was sitting on the bed, his feet dangling over the carpet. He turned to the monk and said, 'In antiquity, a certain happy man grew scared of his own good fortune in the end, it was so immense. So, to propitiate the Gods, he sacrificed his favourite ring. Do you know that I myself, like Polycrates, am getting rather uneasy about my own good fortune? It seems strange that from morning to night I feel only joy, it fills my whole being and stifles all other feelings. As for sorrow, sadness or boredom, I just don't know what they are. Here I am, unable to sleep, suffering from insomnia, but I'm not bored. Seriously, I'm beginning to wonder what it all means.'

'But why?' the monk said in astonishment. 'Is joy something supernatural? Shouldn't it be looked on as man's normal state? The higher man's intellectual and moral development, the freer he is and the more pleasure life gives him. Socrates, Diogenes and Marcus Aurelius experienced joy, not sadness. And the Apostle says, "Rejoice ever more." So rejoice and be happy.'

'But supposing the Gods suddenly became angry?' Kovrin said jokingly and burst out laughing. 'If they were to take my comforts away and make me freeze and starve I don't think I would like that.'

Meanwhile Tanya had woken up and she looked at her husband in horror and bewilderment. He was talking to the armchair, laughing and gesticulating. His eyes shone and there was something peculiar in his laughter.

'Andrey, who are you talking to?' she asked, clutching the hand he had held out to the monk. 'Andrey, who is it?'

'What? Who?' Kovrin said, taken aback. 'Well, to *him* ... He's sitting over there,' he said, pointing at the black monk.

'There's no one here ... no one! Andrey, you're ill!'

Tanya embraced her husband and pressed herself against him, as if to protect him from ghosts and covered his eyes with her hand. 'You're ill!' she sobbed, shaking all over. 'Forgive me, my dearest, but for some time now I've noticed something's wrong with you. You're sick in your mind, Andrey . . .'

Her trembling infected him as well. He looked once more at the armchair, which was empty now and felt a sudden weakness in his arms and legs. This frightened him and he started to dress.

'It's nothing, Tanya, nothing,' he muttered, trembling. 'But to tell the truth, I am a little unwell . . . it's time I admitted it.'

'I noticed it some time ago . . . and Papa did too,' she said, trying to hold back her sobs. 'You talk to yourself, you smile so strangely . . . you're not sleeping. Oh, good God, good God, save us!' she said in horror. 'But don't be afraid, Andrey dear, don't be afraid. For God's sake don't be afraid . . .'

She began to dress too. Only now, as he looked at her, did Kovrin fully realize how dangerous his position was, only now did he understand the meaning of the black monk and his talks with him. He was quite convinced now that he was insane.

Both of them got dressed, without understanding why, and went into the ballroom, she first and he following. And there stood Pesotsky (he was staying with them and had been awakened by the sobbing) in his dressing-gown, with a candle in his hand.

'Don't be afraid, Andrey,' Tanya said, shaking as though in a fever. 'Don't be afraid . . . Papa, it will pass . . . it will pass . . .'

Kovrin could not speak, he was so upset. He wanted to tell his father-in-law, just for a joke, 'Please congratulate me, I think I've gone mad . . .', but all he could do was move his lips and smile bitterly.

At nine in the morning they put his greatcoat and furs on, wrapped a shawl round him and took him in a carriage to the doctor's. He began a course of treatment.

7

Summer had come and the doctor ordered him into the country. Kovrin was better now, had stopped seeing the black monk and it only remained for him to get his strength back. Living with his father-in-law in the country, he drank a lot of milk, worked only two hours a day, and did not drink or smoke.

On the eve of Elijah's Day evening service was held in the house. When the lay reader handed the priest the censer, the enormous old ballroom smelt like a graveyard. Kovrin grew bored. He went out into the garden, wandered about without noticing the gorgeous flowers, sat down on a bench, and then strolled through the park. When he reached the river he went down the slope and stood looking thoughtfully at the water. The gloomy pines with their shaggy roots which had seen him here the previous year looking so young, joyful and lively, no longer talked in whispers, but stood motionless and dumb, as though they did not recognize him. And in fact his hair had been cut short, it was no longer beautiful, he walked sluggishly and his face had grown fuller and paler since the previous summer.

He crossed the foot-bridge to the other side. Where rye had been growing last year were rows of reaped oats. The sun had already set and a broad red glow burned on the horizon, a sign that it would be windy next day. It was quiet. Looking hard in the direction where the black monk had first appeared last year, Kovrin stood for about twenty minutes until the evening glow began to fade.

When he returned to the house, feeling listless and dissatisfied, the service was over. Pesotsky and Tanya were sitting on the terrace steps drinking tea. They were discussing something, but suddenly became silent when they saw Kovrin, and he guessed from their expressions that they had been talking about him.

'Well, I think it's time for your milk,' Tanya told her husband.

'No, it's not,' he answered, sitting on the lowest step. 'Drink it yourself, I don't want any.'

Tanya anxiously exchanged glances with her father and said quietly, 'But you yourself said the milk does you a lot of good!'

'Yes, a lot of good!' Kovrin replied, grinning. 'I congratulate you – since Friday I've put on another pound.' He firmly clasped his head and said in an anguished voice, 'Why, why did you try to cure me? All those bromides, idleness, warm baths, supervision, the cowardly fear with every mouthful, every step. All this will finally turn me into a complete idiot. I was going out of my mind, I had megalomania, but I was bright and cheerful, even happy. I was interesting and original. Now I've grown more rational and stable, but I'm just like everyone else, a nobody. Life bores me ... Oh, how cruelly you've treated me! I did have hallucinations, but did they harm anyone? Who did they harm, that's what I'd like to know?'

'God knows what you're talking about!' Pesotsky sighed. 'It's downright boring listening to you.'

'Then don't listen.'

Kovrin found other people's presence, especially Pesotsky's, irritating and he would answer him drily, coldly, rudely even; and he could not look at him without a feeling of hatred and mockery, which embarrassed Pesotsky, who would cough guiltily, although he didn't feel he was in the least to blame. Unable to understand why their friendly, loving relationship had changed so suddenly, Tanya pressed close to her father and looked him anxiously in the eye. She wanted to understand, but she could not, and she could only see that with every day relations were getting worse, that her father had aged considerably recently, while her husband had become irritable, moody, quarrelsome and uninteresting. No longer could she laugh and sing, she ate nothing at mealtimes, and lay awake whole nights expecting something terrible. She went through such torture that once she lay in a faint from lunch until the evening. During the service she thought that her father was crying and now, when the three of them sat on the terrace, she endeavoured not to think about it.

'How fortunate Buddha, Muhammad or Shakespeare were in not being treated by kind-hearted relatives for ecstasy and

35

inspiration!' Kovrin said. 'If Muhammad had taken potassium bromide for his nerves, had worked only two hours a day and drunk milk, then that remarkable man would have left as much to posterity as his dog. In the long run doctors and kind relatives will turn humanity into a lot of morons. Mediocrity will pass for genius and civilization will perish. If only you knew,' Kovrin added with annoyance, 'how grateful I am to you!'

He was absolutely infuriated and quickly got up and went into the house, in case he said too much. It was quiet and the smell of tobacco flowers and jalap drifted in from the garden through the open windows. Green patches of moonlight lay on the floor in the huge dark ballroom and on the grand piano. Kovrin recalled the joys of the previous summer, when there was that same smell of jalap, and the moon had shone through the windows. Trying to recapture that mood he hurried to his study, lit a strong cigar and told a servant to bring him some wine. But the cigar left a bitter, disgusting taste and the wine tasted differently from last year: these were the effects of having given up the habit. The cigar and two mouthfuls of wine made his head go round, he had palpitations, for which he had to take potassium bromide.

Before she went to bed Tanya told him, 'Father adores you. You're cross with him about something and this is killing him. Just look, he's ageing by the hour, not by the day. I beg you, Andrey, for God's sake, for the sake of your late father, for the sake of my peace of mind, *please* be nice to him!'

'I can't and I won't!'

'But why not?' Tanya asked, trembling all over. 'Tell me, why not?'

'Because I don't like him, that's all,' Kovrin said nonchalantly, with a shrug of the shoulders. 'But let's not talk about him, he's *your* father.'

'I just can't understand, I really can't!' Tanya said, clutching her temples and staring fixedly at something. 'Something incomprehensible and horrible is going on in this house. You've changed, you're not your normal self. A clever, remarkable man like you losing your temper over trifles, getting mixed up in petty squabbles ... These little things worry you and sometimes I'm simply amazed, I just can't believe it's really you.' Then she continued, frightened of her own words and kissing his hands, 'Now, now, don't be angry, don't be angry. You are a clever man, and a good man. You will be fair to father, he's so kind.'

'He's not kind, only smug. Music-hall clowns like your father, bounteous old cranks, with their well-fed, smug faces, used to touch and amuse me once in stories, farces and in real life. But now I find them repugnant. They're egotists to the marrow. What I find most disgusting is their being so well fed, with that optimism that comes from a full belly. They're just like oxen or wild pigs.'

Tanya sat on the bed and laid her head on the pillow. 'This is sheer torture,' she said and from her voice it was plain that she was utterly exhausted and that she found it hard to speak. 'Not a single moment's peace since winter ... It's so terrible. Oh God, I feel shocking!'

'Yes, of course I'm the monster and you and your daddy are the sweet innocents. Of course!'

His face seemed ugly and unpleasant to Tanya. Hatred 37

and that mocking expression did not suit him. And she had in fact noticed before that there was something lacking in his face, as if that had changed too since his hair was cut short. She wanted to say something to hurt him, but immediately she became aware of this hostile feeling she grew frightened and left the bedroom.

8

Kovrin was awarded a professorship. His inaugural lecture was fixed for 2 December and a notice announcing it was put up in the university corridor. But on the appointed day he cabled the dean, informing him he was not well enough to lecture.

He had a haemorrhage in the throat. He would spit blood, but twice a month there was considerable loss of blood, which left him extremely weak and drowsy. The illness did not frighten him particularly, since he knew his late mother had lived with exactly the same disease for ten years or more. And the doctors assured him it was not dangerous, and merely advised him not to get excited, lead a regular life and to talk as little as possible.

In January the lecture was again cancelled for the same reason and in February it was too late to start the course, which had to be postponed until the following year.

He no longer lived with Tanya, but with another woman two years older than he was and who cared for him as though he were a child. His state of mind was calm, submissive. He eagerly gave in to her and when Barbara (his mistress's name) decided to take him to the Crimea he agreed, although he expected no good to come from the trip.

They reached Sevastopol one evening and rested at a hotel before going on to Yalta the next day. They were both exhausted from the journey. Barbara drank some tea, went to bed and soon fell asleep. But Kovrin did not go to bed. Before he had left home – an hour before setting off for the station – he had received a letter from Tanya and had decided not to open it. It was now in one of his coat pockets and the thought of it had a disagreeable, unsettling effect on him. In the very depths of his heart he now considered his marriage to Tanya had been a mistake, and was pleased he had finally broken with her. The memory of that woman who had ended up as a walking skeleton and in whom everything seemed to have died – except for those large, clever, staring eyes – this memory aroused only pity in him and annoyance with himself. The writing on the envelope reminded him how unjust and cruel he had been two years ago, how he had taken revenge on others for his spiritual emptiness, his boredom, his loneliness, his dissatisfaction with life.

In this respect he remembered how he had once torn his dissertation and all the articles written during his illness into shreds and thrown them out of the window, the scraps of paper fluttering in the breeze, catching on trees and flowers. In every line he saw strange, utterly unfounded claims, enthusiasm run riot, audacity and megalomania, which had made him feel as if he were reading a description of his own vices. But when the last notebook had been torn up and had   39 flown through the window, he felt for some reason bitterly annoyed; he had gone to his wife and told her many unpleasant things. God, how he had tormented her! Once, when he wanted to hurt his wife, he told her that her father had played a most distasteful role in their romance, having asked him if he would marry her. Pesotsky happened to hear this and rushed into the room speechless from despair; all he could do was stamp his feet and make a strange bellowing noise, as if he had lost the power of speech, while Tanya looked at her father, gave a heart-rending shriek and fainted. It was an ugly scene.

All this came to mind at the sight of the familiar handwriting. Kovrin went out onto the balcony. The weather was warm and calm, and he could smell the sea. The magnificent bay reflected the moon and the lights, and its colour was hard to describe. It was a delicate, soft blending of dark-blue and green; in places the water was like blue vitriol, in others the moonlight seemed to have taken on material substance and filled the bay instead of water. But what a harmony of colour, what a peaceful, calm and ennobling mood reigned over all!

The windows were most probably open in the room below, beneath the balcony, as he could hear women's voices and laughter quite distinctly. Someone was having a party, it seemed.

Kovrin forced himself to open the letter, returned to his room and read: 'Father has just died. I owe that to you, as you killed him. Our garden is going to rack and ruin – strangers are running it – that's to say, what poor father feared so much has come about. I owe this to you as well. I hate you with all my heart and hope you'll soon be dead. Oh, how I'm suffering! An unbearable pain is burning inside me.

May you be damned! I took you for an outstanding man, for a genius, I loved you, but you turned out a madman . . .'

Kovrin could not read any more, tore the letter up and threw it away. He was seized by a feeling of anxiety that was very close to terror. Barbara was sleeping behind a screen and he could hear her breathing. From the ground floor came women's voices and laughter, but he felt that besides himself there wasn't a living soul in the whole hotel. He was terrified because the unhappy, broken-hearted Tanya had cursed him in her letter and had wished for his death. He glanced at the door, as if fearing that the unknown force which had wrought such havoc in his life and in the lives of those near and dear over the last two years might come into the room and take possession of him again.

He knew from experience that the best cure for shattered nerves is work. One should sit down at a table and force oneself at all costs to concentrate on one idea, no matter what. From his red briefcase he took out a notebook in which he had sketched out a plan for a short work he had considered compiling in case he was bored doing nothing in the Crimea. He sat at the table and started work on the plan and it seemed his calm, resigned, detached state of mind was returning. The notebook and plan even stimulated him to meditate on the world's vanity. He thought how much life demands in return for those insignificant or very ordinary blessings that it can bestow. For example, to receive a university chair in one's late thirties, to be a run-of-the-mill professor, expounding in turgid, boring, ponderous language commonplace ideas that were not even original, in brief, to achieve the status of a 41 third-rate scholar he, Kovrin, had had to study fifteen years – working day and night – suffer severe mental illness, experience a broken marriage and do any number of stupid, unjust things that were best forgotten. Kovrin realized quite clearly now that he was a nobody and eagerly accepted the fact since, in his opinion, every man should be content with what he is.

The plan would have calmed his nerves, but the sight of the shiny white pieces of letter on the floor stopped him concentrating. He got up from the table, picked up the pieces and threw them out of the window, but a light breeze blew in from the sea and scattered them over the window-sill. Once again he was gripped by that restless feeling, akin to panic, and he began to think that there was no one else besides him in the whole hotel . . . He went out onto the balcony. The bay, which seemed to be alive, looked at him with its many sky-blue, dark-blue, turquoise and flame-coloured eyes and beckoned him. It was truly hot and humid, and a bathe would not have come amiss. A violin began to play on the ground floor, under his balcony, and two female voices softly sang a song he knew. It was about some young girl, sick in her mind, who heard mysterious sounds one night in her garden and thought it must be a truly divine harmony, incomprehensible to us mortals . . . Kovrin caught his breath, he felt twinges of sadness in his heart and a wonderful, sweet, long-forgotten gladness quivered in his heart.

A tall black column like a whirlwind or tornado appeared on the far side of the bay. With terrifying speed it moved over the water towards the hotel, growing smaller and darker as it approached, and Kovrin barely had time to move out of

its path . . . Barefoot, arms folded over chest, with a bare grey head and black eyebrows, the monk floated past and stopped in the middle of the room.

'Why didn't you trust me?' he asked reproachfully, looking affectionately at Kovrin. 'If you had trusted me then, when I told you that you were a genius, you wouldn't have spent these two years so miserably, so unprofitably.'

Kovrin believed now that he was one of God's Chosen, and a genius, and he vividly recollected all his previous conversations with the black monk; he wanted to speak, but the blood welled out of his throat onto his chest. Not knowing what to do, he drew his hands over his chest and his shirt cuffs became soaked with blood. He wanted to call Barbara, who was sleeping behind the screen and with a great effort murmured, 'Tanya!'

He fell on the floor, lifted himself on his arms and called again, 'Tanya!'

He called on Tanya, on the great garden with its gorgeous flowers sprinkled with dew, he called on the park, the pines with their shaggy roots, the rye-field, his wonderful learning, his youth, his daring, his joy; he called on life, which had been so beautiful. On the floor near his face, he saw a large pool of blood and was too weak now to say one word, but an ineffable, boundless happiness flooded his whole being. Beneath the balcony they were playing a serenade, and at the same time the black monk whispered to him that he was a genius and that he was dying only because his weak human body had lost its balance and could no longer serve to house a genius. When Barbara woke and came out from behind the screen Kovrin was dead and a blissful smile was frozen on his face.

Peasants

I

Nikolay Chikildeyev, a waiter at the Slav Fair in Moscow, was taken ill. His legs went numb and it affected his walk so much that one day he stumbled and fell down as he was carrying a tray of peas and ham along one of the passages. As a result, he had to give up his job. Any money he and his wife had managed to save went on medical expenses, so they now had nothing to live on. He got bored without a job, so he decided it was probably best to return to his native village. It's easier being ill at home – and it's cheaper; they don't say 'there's no place like home' for nothing.

It was late in the afternoon when he reached his village, Zhukovo. He had always remembered his old home from childhood as a cheerful, bright, cosy, comfortable place, but now, as he entered the hut, he was actually scared when he saw how dark, crowded and filthy it was in there. Olga, his wife, and his daughter, Sasha, who had travelled back with him, stared in utter bewilderment at the huge neglected stove (it took up nearly half the hut), black with soot and flies – so many flies! It was tilting to one side, the wall-beams were all askew, and the hut seemed about to collapse any minute. Instead of pictures, labels from bottles and newspaper-cuttings had been pasted over the wall next to the ikons. This was *real* poverty! All the adults were out reaping. A fair-haired, dirty-faced little girl of about eight was sitting on the stove, so bored she didn't even look up as they came in.

Down below, a white cat was rubbing itself on the fire-irons. Sasha tried to tempt it over: 'Here Puss, here!'

'She can't hear you,' the little girl said, 'she's deaf.'

'How's that?'

'They beat her.'

From the moment they entered the hut, Nikolay and Olga could see the kind of life they led there. But they didn't make any comment, threw their bundles on to the floor and went out into the street without a word. Their hut was third from the end and seemed the poorest and oldest. The second hut was not much better, while the last one – the village inn – had an iron roof and curtains, was unfenced and stood apart from the others. The huts formed a single row and the whole peaceful, sleepy little village, with willows, elders and ash peeping out of the yards, had a pleasant look.

Beyond the gardens, the ground sloped steeply down to the river, like a cliff, with huge boulders sticking out of the clay. Paths threaded their way down the slope between the boulders and pits dug out by the potters, and bits of brown and red clay piled up in great heaps. Down below a bright green, broad and level meadow opened out – it had already been mown and the village cattle were grazing on it. The meandering river with its magnificent leafy banks was almost a mile from the village and beyond were more broad pastures, cattle, long strings of white geese, and then a similar steep slope on its far side. At the top stood a village, a church with five 'onion' domes, with the manor-house a little further on.

'What a lovely spot!' Olga said, crossing herself when she saw the church. 'Heavens, so much open space!'

Just then the bells rang for evensong (it was Saturday evening). Two little girls, who were carrying a bucket of water down the hill, looked back at the church to listen to them.

'It'll be dinner time at the Slav Fair now,' Nikolay said dreamily.

Nikolay and Olga sat on the edge of the cliff, watching the sun go down and the reflections of the gold and crimson sky in the river, in the church windows, in the air all around, which was gentle, tranquil, pure beyond description – such air you never get in Moscow.

But after the sun had set and the lowing cows and bleating sheep had gone past, the geese had flown back from the far side of the river and everything had grown quiet – that gentle light faded from the air and the shades of evening swiftly closed in.

Meanwhile the old couple – Nikolay's parents – had returned. They were skinny, hunchbacked, toothless and the same height. Marya and Fyokla, his sisters-in-law, who worked for a landowner on the other side of the river, had returned too. Marya – the wife of his brother Kiryak – had six children, while Fyokla (married to Denis, who was away on military service) had two. When Nikolay came into the hut and saw all the family there, all those bodies large and small sprawling around on their bunks, cradles, in every corner; when he saw how ravenously the old man and the woman ate their black bread, dipping it first in water, he realized that he had made a mistake coming here, ill as he was, without any

money and with his family into the bargain – a real blunder!

'And where's my brother Kiryak?' he asked when they had greeted each other.

'He's living in the forest, working as a night watchman for some merchant. Not a bad sort, but he can't half knock it back!'

'He's no breadwinner!' the old woman murmured tearfully. 'Our men are a lousy lot of drunkards, they don't bring their money back home! Kiryak's a drinker. And the old man knows the way to the pub as well, there's no harm in saying it! The Blessed Virgin must have it in for us!'

They put the samovar on especially for the guests. The tea smelled of fish, the sugar was grey and had been nibbled at, and cockroaches ran all over the bread and crockery. The tea was revolting, just like the conversation, which was always about illness and how they had no money. But before they even managed to drink the first cup a loud, long drawn-out, drunken cry came from outside.

'Ma-arya!'

'Sounds like Kiryak's back,' the old man said. 'Talk of the devil.'

Everyone went quiet. And a few moments later they heard that cry again, coarse and drawling, as though it was coming from under the earth.

'Ma-arya!'

Marya, the elder sister, turned pale and huddled closer to the stove, and it was somehow strange to see fear written all over the face of that strong, broad-shouldered woman. Suddenly her daughter – the same little girl who had been sitting over the stove looking so apathetic – sobbed out loud.

47

'And what's the matter with you, you silly cow?' Fyokla shouted at her – she was strong and broad-shouldered as well. 'I don't suppose he's going to kill you.'

Nikolay learned from the old man that Marya didn't live in the forest, as she was scared of Kiryak, and that whenever he was drunk he would come after her, make a great racket and always beat her mercilessly.

'Ma-arya!' came the cry – this time right outside the door.

'Please, help me, for Christ's sake, my own dear ones . . .' Marya mumbled breathlessly, panting as though she had just been dropped into freezing water. 'Please protect me . . .'

Every single child in the hut burst out crying, and Sasha gave them one look and followed suit. There was a drunken coughing, and a tall man with a black beard and a fur cap came into the hut. As his face was not visible in the dim lamplight, he was quite terrifying. It was Kiryak. He went over to his wife, swung his arm and hit her across the face with his fist. She was too stunned to cry out and merely sank to the ground; the blood immediately gushed from her nose.

'Should be ashamed of yourself, bloody ashamed!' the old man muttered as he climbed up over the stove. 'And in front of guests. A damned disgrace!'

But the old woman sat there without saying a word, all hunched up, and seemed to be thinking; Fyokla went on rocking the cradle. Clearly pleased at the terrifying effect he had on everyone, Kiryak seized Marya's hand, dragged her to the door and howled like a wild animal, so that he seemed even more terrifying. But then he suddenly saw the guests

and stopped short in his tracks.

'Oh, so you've arrived . . .' he muttered, letting go of his wife. 'My own brother, with family and all . . .'

He reeled from side to side as he said a prayer in front of the ikon, and his drunken red eyes were wide open. Then he continued, 'So my dear brother's come back home with his family . . . from Moscow. The great capital, that is, Moscow, mother of cities . . . Forgive me . . .'

He sank down on a bench by the samovar and started drinking tea, noisily gulping from a saucer, while no one else said a word. He drank about ten cups, then slumped down on the bench and started snoring.

They prepared for bed. As Nikolay was ill, they put him over the stove with the old man. Sasha lay down on the floor, while Olga went into the barn with the other women.

'Well, dear,' Olga said, lying down on the straw next to Marya. 'It's no good crying. You've got to grin and bear it. The Bible says: "Whosoever shall smite thee on the right cheek, turn to him the other also . . ." Yes, dear!'

Then she told her about her life in Moscow, in a whispering, sing-song voice, about her job as a maid in some furnished flats.

'The houses are very big there and built of stone,' she said. 'There's ever so many churches – scores and scores of them, my dear, and them that live in the houses are all gentlefolk, so handsome and respectable!'

Marya replied that she had never been further than the county town, let alone Moscow. She was illiterate, did not know any prayers – even 'Our Father'. Both she and Fyokla, the other sister-in-law, who was sitting not very far away, 49 listening, were extremely backward and understood nothing. Neither loved her husband. Marya was frightened of Kiryak and whenever he stayed with her she would tremble all over. And he stank so much of tobacco and vodka she nearly went out of her mind. If anyone asked Fyokla if she got bored when her husband was away, she would reply indignantly, 'to hell with him!' They kept talking a little longer and then fell silent . . .

It was cool and they could not sleep because of a cock crowing near the barn for all it was worth. When the hazy-blue light of morning was already filtering through every chink in the woodwork, Fyokla quietly got up and went outside. Then they heard her running off somewhere, her bare feet thudding over the ground.

2

Olga went to church, taking Marya with her. Both of them felt cheerful as they went down the path to the meadow. Olga liked the wide-open spaces, while Marya sensed that her sister-in-law was someone near and dear to her. The sun was rising and a sleepy hawk flew low over the meadows. The river looked gloomy, with patches of mist here and there. But a strip of sunlight already stretched along the hill on the far side of the river, the church shone brightly and crows cawed furiously in the manor-house garden.

'The old man's all right,' Marya was telling her, 'only Grannie's very strict and she's always on the warpath. Our own bread lasted until Shrovetide, then we had to go and buy some flour at the inn. That put her in a right temper, said we were eating too much.'

'Oh, what of it, dear! You just have to grin and bear it. As it says in the Bible: "Come unto me, all ye that labour and are heavy laden."'

Olga had a measured, sing-song voice and she walked like a pilgrim, quick and bustling. Every day she read out loud from the Gospels, like a priest, and there was much she did not understand. However, the sacred words moved her to tears and she pronounced 'if whomsoever' and 'whither' with a sweet sinking feeling in her heart. She believed in God, the Holy Virgin and the saints. She believed that it was wrong to harm anyone in the wide world – whether they were simple people, Germans, gipsies or Jews – and woe betide those who were cruel to animals! She believed that all this was written down in the sacred books and this was why, when she repeated words from the Bible – even words she did not understand – her face became compassionate, radiant and full of tenderness.

'Where are you from?' Marya asked.

'Vladimir. But my parents took me with them to Moscow a long time ago, when I was only eight.'

They went down to the river. On the far side a woman stood at the water's edge, undressing herself.

'That's our Fyokla,' Marya said, recognizing her. 'She's been going across the river to the manor-house to lark around with the men. She's a real tart and you should hear her swear – something wicked!'

Fyokla, who had black eyebrows and who still had the youthfulness and strength of a young girl, leapt from the bank into the water, her hair undone, threshing the water with her legs and sending out ripples in all directions.

'A real tart!' Marya said again.

Over the river was a rickety wooden plank footbridge and right below it shoals of large-headed chub swam in the pure, clear water. Dew glistened on green bushes which seemed to be looking at themselves in the river. A warm breeze was blowing and everything became so pleasant. What a beautiful morning! And how beautiful life could be in this world, were it not for all its terrible, never-ending poverty, from which there is no escape! One brief glance at the village brought yesterday's memories vividly to life – and that enchanting happiness, which seemed to be all around, vanished in a second.

They reached the church. Marya stopped at the porch, not daring to go in, or even sit down, although the bells for evening service would not ring until after eight. So she just kept standing there.

During the reading from the Gospels, the congregation suddenly moved to one side to make way for the squire and his family. Two girls in white frocks and broad-brimmed hats and a plump, pink-faced boy in a sailor suit came down the church. Olga was very moved when she saw them and was immediately convinced that these were respectable, well-educated, fine people. But Marya gave them a suspicious, dejected look, as though they were not human beings but monsters who would trample all over her if she did not get out of the way. And whenever the priest's deep voice thundered out, she imagined she could hear that shout again – *Ma-arya!* – and she trembled all over.

3

The villagers heard about the newly arrived visitors and a large crowd was already waiting in the hut after the service. Among them were the Leonychevs, the Matveichevs and the Ilichovs, who wanted news of their relatives working in Moscow. All the boys from Zhukovo who could read or write were bundled off to Moscow to be waiters or bellboys (the lads from the village on the other side of the river just became bakers). This was a long-standing practice, going back to the days of serfdom when a certain peasant from Zhukovo called Luka (now a legend) had worked as a barman in a Moscow club and only took on people who came from his own village. Once these villagers had made good, they in turn sent for their families and fixed them up with jobs in pubs and restaurants. Ever since then, the village of Zhukovo had always been called 'Loutville' or 'Lackeyville' by the locals. Nikolay had been sent to Moscow when he was eleven and he got a job through Ivan (one of the Matveichevs), who was then working as an usher at the 'Hermitage' Gardens. Rather didactically Nikolay told the Matveichevs, 'Ivan was very good to me, so I must pray for him night and day. It was through him I became a good man.'

Ivan's sister, a tall old lady, said tearfully, 'Yes, my dear friend, we don't hear anything from them these days.'

'Last winter he was working at Aumont's,* but they say he's out of town now, working in some suburban pleasure gardens. He's aged terribly. Used to take home ten roubles a day in the summer season. But business is slack everywhere now, the old boy doesn't know what to do with himself.'

The woman looked at Nikolay's legs (he was wearing felt boots), at his pale face and sadly said, 'You're no breadwinner, Nikolay. How can you be, in your state!'

They all made a fuss of Sasha. She was already ten years old, but she was short for her age, very thin and no one would have thought she was more than seven, at the very most. This fair-haired girl with her big dark eyes and a red ribbon in her hair looked rather comical among the others, with their deeply tanned skin, crudely cut hair and their long faded smocks – she resembled a small animal that had been caught in a field and brought into the hut.

'And she knows how to read!' Olga said boastfully as she tenderly looked at her daughter. 'Read something, dear!' she said, taking a Bible from one corner. 'You read a little bit and these good Christians will listen.'

The Bible was old and heavy, bound in leather and with well-thumbed pages; it smelled as though some monks had come into the hut. Sasha raised her eyebrows and began reading in a loud, singing voice, 'And when they were departed, behold, the angel of the Lord . . . appeared to Joseph in a dream, saying, "Arise, and take the young child and his mother."'

* Aumont's, a well-known amusement house.

' "The young child and his mother",' Olga repeated and became flushed with excitement.

' "And flee into Egypt . . . and be thou there until I bring thee word . . ." '

At the word 'until', Olga broke down and wept. Marya looked at her and started sobbing, and Ivan's sister followed suit. Then the old man had a fit of coughing and fussed around trying to find a present for his little granddaughter. But he could not find anything and finally gave it up as a bad job. After the reading, the neighbours went home, deeply touched and extremely pleased with Olga and Sasha.

When there was a holiday the family would stay at home all day. The old lady, called 'Grannie' by her husband, daughters-in-law and grandchildren, tried to do all the work herself. She would light the stove, put the samovar on, go to milk the cows and then complain she was worked to death. She kept worrying that someone might eat a little too much or that the old man and the daughters-in-law might have no work to do. One moment she would be thinking that she could hear the innkeeper's geese straying into her kitchen garden from around the back, and she would dash out of the hut with a long stick and stand screaming for half an hour on end by her cabbages that were as withered and stunted as herself; and then she imagined a crow was stalking her chickens and she would rush at it, swearing for all she was worth. She would rant and rave from morning to night and very often her shouting was so loud that people stopped in the street.

She did not treat the old man with much affection and 55

called him 'lazy devil' or 'damned nuisance'. He was frivolous and unreliable and wouldn't have done any work at all (most likely he would have sat over the stove all day long, talking) if his wife hadn't continually prodded him. He would spend hours on end telling his son stories about his enemies and complaining about the daily insults he had apparently to suffer from his neighbours. It was very boring listening to him.

'Oh yes,' he would say, holding his sides. 'Yes, a week after Exaltation of the Cross, I sold some hay at thirty kopeks a third of a hundredweight, just what I wanted . . . Yes, very good business. But one morning, as I was carting the hay, keeping to myself, not interfering with anyone . . . it was my rotten luck that Antip Sedelnikov, the village elder, comes out of the pub and asks: "Where you taking that lot, you devil . . .?" and he gives me one on the ear.'

Kiryak had a terrible hangover and he felt very shamed in front of his brother.

'That's what you get from drinking vodka,' he muttered, shaking his splitting head. 'Oh God! My own brother and sister-in-law! Please forgive me, for Christ's sake. I'm so ashamed!'

For the holidays they bought some herring at the inn and made soup from the heads. At midday they sat down to tea and went on drinking until the sweat poured off them. They looked puffed out with all that liquid and after the tea they started on the soup, everyone drinking from the same pot. Grannie had what was left of the herring.

That evening a potter was firing clay on the side of the

cliff. In the meadows down below, girls were singing and dancing in a ring. Someone was playing an accordion. Another kiln had been lit across the river and the girls there were singing as well and their songs were soft and melodious in the distance. At the inn and round about, some peasants were making a great noise with their discordant singing and they swore so much that Olga could only shudder and exclaim, 'Oh, good heavens!'

She was astonished that the swearing never stopped for one minute and that the old men with one foot in the grave were the ones who swore loudest and longest. But the children and the young girls were obviously used to it from the cradle and it did not worry them at all.

Now it was past midnight and the fires in the pottery kilns on both sides of the river had gone out. But the festivities continued in the meadow below and at the inn. The old man and Kiryak, both drunk, joined arms and kept bumping into each other as they went up to the barn where Olga and Marya were lying.

'Leave her alone,' the old man urged Kiryak. 'Let her be. She doesn't do any harm . . . it's *shameful* . . .'

'Ma-arya!' Kiryak shouted.

'Leave her alone . . . it's sinful . . . she's not a bad woman.'

They both paused for a moment near the barn, then they moved on.

'I lo-ove the flowers that bloom in the fields, oh!' the old man suddenly struck up in his shrill, piercing tenor voice. 'Oh, I do lo-ove to pick the flo-owers!'

Then he spat, swore obscenely and went into the hut.

Grannie stationed Sasha near her kitchen garden and told her to watch out for stray geese. It was a hot August day. The geese could have got into the garden from round the back, but now they were busily pecking at some oats near the inn, peacefully cackling to each other. Only the gander craned his neck, as though he were looking out for the old woman with her stick. The other geese might have come up from the slope, but they stayed far beyond the other side of the river and resembled a long white garland of flowers laid out over the meadow.

Sasha stood there for a few moments, after which she felt bored. When she saw that the geese weren't coming, off she went down the steep slope. There she spotted Motka (Marya's eldest daughter), standing motionless on a boulder, looking at the church. Marya had borne thirteen children, but only six survived, all of them girls – not a single boy among them; and the eldest was eight. Motka stood barefooted in her long smock, in the full glare of the sun which burned down on her head. But she did not notice it and seemed petrified. Sasha stood next to her and said as she looked at the church, 'God lives in churches. People have ikon lamps and candles, but God has little red, green and blue lamps that are just like tiny eyes. At night-time God goes walking round the church with the Holy Virgin and Saint Nikolay . . . tap-tap-tap. And the watchman is scared stiff!' Then she added, mimicking her mother, 'Now, dear, when the Day of Judgement comes, every church will be whirled off to heaven!'

'Wha-at, with their be-ells too?' Motka asked in a deep voice, dragging each syllable.

'Yes, bells and all. On the Day of Judgement, all good people will go to paradise, while the wicked ones will be burnt in everlasting fire, for ever and ever. And God will tell my mother and Marya, "You never harmed anyone, so you can take the path on the right that leads to paradise." But he'll say to Kiryak and Grannie, "You go to the left, into the fire. And all those who ate meat during Lent must go as well."'

She gazed up at the sky with wide-open eyes and said, 'If you look at the sky without blinking you can see the angels.'

Motka looked upwards and neither of them said a word for a minute or so.

'Can you see them?' Sasha asked.

'Can't see nothing,' Motka said in her deep voice.

'Well, *I* can. There's tiny angels flying through the sky, flapping their wings and going buzz-buzz like mosquitoes.'

Motka pondered for a moment as she looked down at the ground and then she asked, 'Will Grannie burn in the fire?'

'Yes, she will, dear.'

From the rock down to the bottom, the slope was gentle and smooth. It was covered with soft green grass which made one feel like touching it or lying on it. Sasha lay down and rolled to the bottom. Motka took a deep breath and, looking very solemn and deadly serious, she lay down too and rolled to the bottom; on the way down her smock rode up to her shoulders.

'That was great fun,' Sasha said rapturously.

They both went up to the top again for another roll, but just then they heard that familiar, piercing voice again. It was really terrifying! That toothless, bony, hunchbacked old woman, with her short grey hair fluttering in the wind, was driving the geese out of her kitchen garden with a long stick, shouting, 'So you had to tread all over my cabbages, blast you! May you be damned three times and rot in hell, you buggers!'

When she saw the girls, she threw the stick down, seized a whip made of twigs, gripped Sasha's neck with fingers as hard and dry as stale rolls, and started beating her. Sasha cried out in pain and fear, but at that moment the gander, waddling along and craning its neck, went up to the old woman and hissed at her. When it returned to the flock all the females cackled approvingly. Then the old woman started beating Motka and her smock rode up again. With loud sobs and in utter desperation, Sasha went to the hut to complain about it. She was followed by Motka, who was crying as well, but much more throatily and without bothering to wipe the tears away. Her face was so wet it seemed she had just drenched it with water.

'Good God!' Olga said in astonishment when they entered the hut. 'Holy Virgin!'

Sasha was just about to tell her what had happened when Grannie started shrieking and cursing. Fyokla became furious and the hut was filled with noise. Olga was pale and looked very upset as she stroked Sasha's head and said consolingly, 'It's all right, it's nothing. It's sinful to get angry with your grandmother. It's all right, my child.'

60

Nikolay, who by this time was exhausted by the never-ending shouting, by hunger, by the fumes from the stove and the terrible stench, who hated and despised poverty, and whose wife and daughter made him feel ashamed in front of his parents, sat over the stove with his legs dangling and turned to his mother in an irritable, plaintive voice: 'You can't beat her, you've no right at all!'

'You feeble little man, rotting away up there over the stove,' Fyokla shouted spitefully. 'What the hell's brought you lot here, you parasites!'

Both Sasha and Motka and all the little girls, who had taken refuge in the corner, over the stove, behind Nikolay's back, were terrified and listened without saying a word, their little hearts pounding away.

When someone in a family has been terribly ill for a long time, when all hope has been given up, there are horrible moments when those near and dear to him harbour a timid, secret longing, deep down inside, for him to die. Only children fear the death of a loved one and the very thought of it fills them with terror. And now the little girls held their breath and looked at Nikolay with mournful expressions on their faces, thinking that he would soon be dead. They felt like crying and telling him something tender and comforting.

He clung to Olga, as though seeking protection, and he told her softly, tremulously, 'My dear Olga, I can't stand it any more here. All my strength has gone. For God's sake, for Christ's sake, write to your sister Claudia and tell her to sell or pawn all she has. Then she can send us the money to help us get out of this place.'

He went on in a voice that was full of yearning: 'Oh God, just one glimpse of Moscow is all I ask! If only I just could *dream* about my dear Moscow!'

When evening came and it was dark in the hut, they felt so depressed they could hardly speak. Angry Grannie sat dipping rye-crusts in a cup and sucking them for a whole hour. After Marya had milked the cow she brought a pail of milk and put it on a bench. Then Grannie poured it into some jugs, without hurrying, and she was visibly cheered by the thought that as it was the Feast of the Assumption (when milk was forbidden) no one would go near it. All she did was pour the tiniest little drop into a saucer for Fyokla's baby. As she was carrying the jugs with Marya down to the cellar, Motka suddenly started, slid down from the stove, went over to the bench where the wooden cup with the crusts was standing and splashed some milk from the saucer over them.

When Grannie came back and sat down to her crusts, Sasha and Motka sat watching her from the stove, and it gave them great pleasure to see that now she had eaten forbidden food during Lent and would surely go to hell for it. They took comfort in this thought and lay down to sleep. As Sasha dozed off she had visions of the Day of Judgement; she saw a blazing furnace, like a potter's kiln, and an evil spirit dressed all in black, with the horns of a cow, driving Grannie into the fire with a long stick, as *she* had driven the geese not so long ago.

5

After ten o'clock, on the eve of the Feast of the Assumption, the young men and girls who were strolling in the meadows down below suddenly started shouting and screaming and came running back to the village. People who were sitting up on the hill, on the edge of the cliffs could not understand at first what had happened.

'Fire! Fire!' came the desperate cry from below. 'We're on fire!'

The people up above looked round and were confronted by the most terrifying, extraordinary sight: on the thatched roof of one of the huts at the end of the village a pillar of fire swirled upwards, showering sparks everywhere like a fountain. The whole roof turned into a mass of bright flames and there was a loud crackling. The moonlight was dimmed by the glare and the whole village became enveloped in a red, flickering light. Black shadows stole over the ground and there was a smell of burning. The villagers had come running up the hill, were all out of breath and could not speak for trembling; they jostled each other and kept falling down, unable to see properly in that sudden blinding light and not recognizing one another. It was terrifying, particularly with pigeons flying around in the smoke above the fire, while down at the inn (they had not heard about the fire) the singing and accordion-playing continued as if nothing had happened.

'Uncle Semyon's hut's on fire!' someone shouted in a loud, rough voice.

Marya was dashing around near the hut, crying and wringing her hands and her teeth chattered — even though the fire was some distance away, at the far end of the village.

Nikolay emerged in his felt boots and the children came running out in their little smocks. Some of the villagers banged on an iron plate by the police constable's hut, filling the air with a loud clanging; this incessant, unremitting sound made your heart ache and made you go cold all over.

Old women stood holding ikons.

Sheep, calves and cows were driven out into the street from the yards; trunks, sheepskins and tubs were carried outside. A black stallion, normally kept apart from the herd — it had a tendency to kick and injure the others — was set loose and galloped once or twice through the village, whinnying and stamping, and then suddenly stopped near a cart and lashed out with its hind legs.

And the bells were ringing out in the church on the other side of the river. Near the blazing hut it was hot and so light that the tiniest blade of grass was visible.

Semyon, a red-haired peasant with a large nose, wearing a waistcoat and with his cap pulled down over his ears, was sitting on one of the trunks they had managed to drag out. His wife was lying face downwards moaning in despair. An old man of about eighty, shortish, with an enormous beard — rather like a gnome — and who was obviously in some way connected with the fire (although he came from another village), was pacing up and down without any hat, carrying a white bundle. A bald patch on his head glinted in the light of the fire. Antip Sedelnikov, the village elder — a swarthy man with the black hair of a gipsy – went up to the hut with an axe and, for some obscure reason, knocked out the windows, one after the other. Then he started hacking away at the front steps.

'Get some water, you women!' he shouted. 'Bring the fire-engine! And be quick about it!'

A fire-engine was hauled up by the same villagers who had just been drinking and singing at the inn. They were all dead-drunk and kept stumbling and falling over; all of them had a helpless look and they had tears in their eyes.

The village elder, who was drunk as well, shouted, 'Get some water, quick!'

The women and girls ran down to the bottom of the hill, where there was a spring, dragged up the full buckets and tubs, emptied them into the fire-engine and ran down again. Olga, Marya, Sasha and Motka all helped. The women and little boys helped to pump the water, making the hosepipe hiss, and the village elder began by directing a jet into the doorway, then through the windows, regulating the flow with his finger, which made the water hiss all the more.

'Well done, Antip!' the villagers said approvingly. 'Come on now!'

Antip climbed right into the burning hall from where he shouted, 'Keep on pouring. Try your best, you good Christians, on the occasion of such an unhappy event.'

The villagers crowded round and did nothing – they just gazed at the fire. No one had any idea what to do – no one was capable of doing anything – and close by there were stacks of wheat and hay, piles of dry brushwood, and barns. Kiryak and old Osip, his father, had joined in the crowd, and they were both drunk. The old man turned to the woman lying on the ground and said – as though trying to find some excuse for his idleness – 'Now don't get so worked up! The hut's insured, so don't worry!'

Semyon turned to one villager after the other, telling them how the fire had started.

'It was that old man with the bundle, him what worked for General Zhukov . . . used to cook for him, God rest his soul. Along he comes this evening and says, "Let me stay the night, please." Well, we had a drink or two . . . the old girl started messing around with the samovar to make the old man a cup of tea and she put it in the hall before the charcoal was out. The flames shot straight up out of the pipe and set the thatched roof alight, so there you are! *We* nearly went up as well. The old man's cap was burnt, a terrible shame.'

Meanwhile they banged away at the iron plate for all they were worth and the bells in the church across the river kept ringing. Olga ran breathlessly up and down the slope. As she looked in horror at the red sheep, at the pink doves fluttering around in the smoke, she was lit up by the fierce glow. The loud clanging had the effect of a sharp needle piercing her heart and it seemed that the fire would never go out, that Sasha was lost . . . And when the ceiling in the hut collapsed with a loud crash, the thought that the whole village was bound to burn down now made her feel weak and she could not carry any more water. So she sat on the cliff, with the buckets at her side. Nearby, a little lower down, women were sitting and seemed to be wailing for the dead.

But just then some labourers and men from the manor
across the river arrived in two carts, together with a fire-

engine. A very young student came riding up in his unbuttoned white tunic. Axes started hacking away, a ladder was propped against the blazing framework and five men clambered up it at once, with the student leading the way. His face was red from the flames and he shouted in a hoarse, rasping voice, in such an authoritative way it seemed putting fires out was something he did every day. They tore the hut to pieces beam by beam, and they tore down the cowshed, a wattle fence and the nearest haystack.

Stern voices rang out from the crowd: 'Don't let them smash the place up. Stop them!'

Kiryak went off towards the hut with a determined look and as though intending stopping the newly arrived helpers from breaking the whole place up. But one of the workmen turned him round and hit him in the neck. There was laughter and the workman hit him again. Kiryak fell down and crawled back to the crowd on all fours.

Two pretty girls, wearing hats – they were probably the student's sisters – arrived from across the river. They stood a little way off, watching the fire. The beams that had been pulled down had stopped burning, but a great deal of smoke still came from them. As he manipulated the hose, the student directed the jet at the beams, then at the peasants and then at the women fetching the water.

'Georges!' the girls shouted, in anxious, reproachful voices. 'Georges!'

The fire was out now and only when they started going home did the villagers notice that it was already dawn and that everyone had that pale, slightly swarthy look which 67 always seems to come in the early hours of the morning, when the last stars have faded from the sky. As they went their different ways, the villagers laughed and made fun of General Zhukov's cook and his burnt hat. Already they wanted to turn the fire into a joke – and they even seemed sorry that it was all over so quickly.

'You were a very good fireman,' Olga told the student. 'You should come to Moscow where we live, there's a fire every day.'

'You don't say, you're from *Moscow*?' one of the young ladies asked.

'Oh yes. My husband worked at the Slav Fair. And this is my daughter.'

She pointed to Sasha, who went cold all over and clung to her. 'She's from Moscow as well, Miss.'

The two girls said something in French to the student and he gave Sasha a twenty-kopek piece. When old Osip saw it, there was a sudden flicker of hope on his face.

'Thank God there wasn't any wind, sir,' he said, turning to the student, 'or everything would have gone up before you could say knife.' Then he lowered his voice and added timidly, 'Yes, sir, and you ladies, you're good people . . . it's cold at dawn, could do with warming up . . . Please give me a little something for a drink . . .'

They gave him nothing and he sighed and slunk off home. Afterwards Olga stood at the top of the slope and watched the two carts fording the river and the two ladies and the gentleman riding across the meadow – a carriage was waiting for them on the other side.

When she went back into the hut she told her husband delightedly, 'Such fine people! And so good-looking. Those young ladies were like little cherubs!'

'They can damned well go to hell!' murmured sleepy Fyokla, in a voice full of hatred.

6

Marya was unhappy and said that she longed to die. Fyokla, on the other hand, found this kind of life to her liking – for all its poverty, filth and never-ending bad language. She ate whatever she was given, without any fuss, and slept anywhere she could and on whatever she happened to find. She would empty the slops right outside the front door, splashing them out from the steps, and she would walk barefoot through the puddles into the bargain. From the very first day she had hated Olga and Nikolay, precisely because they did not like the life there.

'We'll see what you get to eat here, my posh Moscow friends,' she said viciously. 'We'll see!'

One morning, right at the beginning of September, the healthy, fine-looking Fyokla, her face flushed with the cold, brought two buckets of water up the hill. Marya and Olga were sitting at the table drinking tea.

'Tea *and* sugar!' Fyokla said derisively. 'Real ladies!' she added, putting the buckets down. 'Is it the latest fashion, then, drinking tea every day? Careful you don't burst with all that liquid inside you.' She gave Olga a hateful look and went 69 on, 'Stuffed your fat mug all right in Moscow, didn't you, you fat cow!'

She swung the yoke and hit Olga on the shoulders; this startled the sisters-in-law so much that all they could do was clasp their hands and say, 'Oh, good heavens!'

Then Fyokla went down to the river to do some washing and she swore so loudly the whole way there, they could hear her back in the hut.

The day drew to a close and the long autumn evening set in. In the hut they were winding silk – everyone, that is, except Fyokla, who had gone across the river.

The silk was collected from a nearby factory and the whole family earned itself a little pocket money – twenty kopeks a week.

'We were better off as serfs,' the old man said as he wound the silk. 'You worked, ate, slept – everything had its proper place. You had cabbage soup and kasha for your dinner and again for supper. You had as many cucumbers and as much cabbage as you liked and you could eat to your heart's content, if you felt like it. And they were stricter then, everyone knew his place.'

Only one lamp was alight, smoking and glowing dimly. Whenever anyone stood in front of it, a large shadow fell across the window and one could see the bright moonlight. Old Osip took his time as he told them all what life was like before the serfs were emancipated;* how, in those very same places where life was so dull and wretched now, they used to

* The serfs were officially emancipated in 1861.

ride out with wolfhounds, borzois and skilled hunters. There would be plenty of vodka for the peasants during the battue. He told how whole cartloads of game were taken to Moscow for the young gentlemen, how badly behaved peasants were flogged or sent away to estates in Tver, while the good ones were rewarded. Grannie had stories to tell as well. She remembered simply everything. She told of her mistress, whose husband was a drunkard and a rake and whose daughters all made absolutely disastrous marriages; one married a drunkard, another a small tradesman in the town, while the third eloped (with the help of Grannie, who was a girl herself at the time). In no time at all they all died of broken hearts (like their mother) and Grannie burst into tears when she recalled it all.

Suddenly there was a knock at the door and everyone trembled.

'Uncle Osip, put me up for tonight, please!'

In came General Zhukov's cook – a bald, little old man, the same cook whose hat had been burnt. He sat down, listened to the conversation and soon joined in, reminiscing and telling stories about the old days. Nikolay sat listening with his legs dangling from the stove and all he wanted to know was what kind of food they used to eat in the days of serfdom. They discussed various kinds of rissoles, cutlets, soups and sauces. The cook, who had a good memory as well, mentioned dishes that were not made any more. For example, there was some dish made from bulls' eyes called *morning awakening*.

'Did they make cutlets *à la maréchale* then?' Nikolay asked.
'No.'

Nikolay shook his head disdainfully and said, 'Oh, you little apology for a cook!'

The little girls who were sitting or lying on the stove looked down without blinking. There seemed to be so many of them, they were like cherubs in the clouds. They liked the stories, sighed, shuddered and turned pale with delight or fear. Breathlessly they listened to Grannie's stories, which were the most interesting, and they were too frightened to move a muscle. All of them lay down to sleep without saying a word. The old people, excited and disturbed by the stories, thought about the beauty of youth, now that it was past: no matter what it had *really* been like, they could only remember it as bright, joyful and moving. And now they thought of the terrible chill of death – and for them death was not far away. Better not to think about it! The lamp went out. The darkness, the two windows sharply outlined in the moonlight, the silence and the creaking cradle somehow reminded them that their lives were finished, nothing could bring them back. Sometimes one becomes drowsy and dozes off, and suddenly someone touches you on the shoulder, breathes on your cheek and you can sleep no longer, your whole body goes numb, and you can think of nothing but death. You turn over and death is forgotten; but then the same old depressing, tedious thoughts keep wandering around your head – thoughts of poverty, cattle fodder, about the higher price of flour and a little later you remember once again that your life has gone, that you can never re-live it.

'Oh God!' sighed the cook.

Someone was tapping ever so gently on the window – that

must be Fyokla. Olga stood up, yawning and whispering a prayer as she opened the door and then drew the bolt back in the hall. But no one came in and there was just a breath of chill air from the street and the sudden bright light of the moon. Through the open door she could see the quiet, deserted street and the moon itself sailing across the heavens.

Olga called out, 'Who is it?'

'It's me,' came the answer, 'it's me.'

Fyokla was standing near the door, pressing close to the wall, and she was stark naked. She was trembling with the cold and her teeth chattered. In the bright moonlight she looked very pale, beautiful and strange. The shadow and the brilliant light playing over her skin struck Olga particularly vividly and those dark eyebrows and firm young breasts were very sharply outlined.

'It was them beasts on the other side of the river, they stripped me naked and sent me away like this ...' she muttered. 'I've come all the way home without nothing on ... stark naked ... Give me some clothes.'

'Come into the hut!' Olga said softly and she too started shivering.

'I don't want the old people to see me!'

But in actual fact Grannie had already become alarmed and was grumbling away, while the old man asked, 'Who's there?'

Olga fetched her own smock and skirt and dressed Fyokla in them. Then they both tiptoed into the hut, trying not to bang the doors.

'Is that you, my beauty?' Grannie growled angrily when   73 she realized who it was. 'You little nightbird, want a nice flogging, do you?'

'It's all right, it's all right, dear,' Olga whispered as she wrapped Fyokla up.

Everything became quiet again. They always slept badly in the hut, every one of them would be kept awake by obsessive, nagging thoughts – the old man by his backache, Grannie by her worrying and evil mind, Marya by her fear and the children by itching and hunger.

And now their sleep was as disturbed as ever and they kept tossing and turning, and saying wild things; time after time they got up for a drink of water.

Suddenly Fyokla started bawling in her loud, coarse voice, but immediately tried to pull herself together and broke into an intermittent sobbing which gradually became fainter and fainter until it died away completely. Now and again the church on the other side of the river could be heard striking the hour, but in the most peculiar way: first it struck five and then three.

'Oh, my God!' sighed the cook.

It was hard to tell, just by looking at the windows, whether the moon was still shining or if dawn had already come. Marya got up and went outside. They could hear her milking the cow in the yard and telling it, 'Ooh, keep still!' Grannie went out as well. Although it was still dark in the hut, by now every object was visible.

Nikolay, who had not slept the whole night, climbed down from the stove. He took his tailcoat out of a green trunk, put it on, smoothed the sleeves as he went over to the window, held the tails for a moment and smiled. Then he carefully took it off, put it back in the trunk and lay down again.

Marya returned and started lighting the stove. Quite clearly she was not really awake yet and she was still coming to as she moved around. Most probably she had had a dream or suddenly remembered the stories of the evening before, since she said, 'No, *freedom** is best,' as she sensuously stretched herself in front of the stove.

7

The 'gentleman' arrived – this was how the local police inspector was called in the village. Everyone knew a week beforehand exactly when and why he was coming. In Zhukovo there were only forty households, but they were so much in arrears with their taxes and rates that over two thousand roubles were overdue.

The inspector stopped at the inn. There he 'imbibed' two glasses of tea and then set off on foot for the village elder's hut, where a crowd of defaulters was waiting for him. Antip Sedelnikov, the village elder, despite his lack of years (he had only just turned thirty) was a very strict man and always sided with the authorities, although he was poor himself and was always behind with his payments. Being the village elder obviously amused him and he enjoyed the feeling of power and the only way he knew to exercise this was by enforcing

* Marya means freedom from serfdom.

strict discipline. At village meetings everyone was scared of him and did what he said. If he came across a drunk in the street or near the inn he would swoop down on him, tie his arms behind his back and put him in the village lock-up. Once he had even put Grannie there for swearing when she was deputizing for Osip at a meeting and he kept her locked up for twenty-four hours. Although he had never lived in a town or read any books, somehow he had managed to accumulate a store of various clever-sounding words and he loved using them in conversation, which made him respected, if not always understood.

When Osip entered the elder's hut with his rent-book, the inspector – a lean old man with long grey whiskers, in a grey double-breasted jacket – was sitting at a table in the corner near the stove, writing something down. The hut was clean and all the walls were gay and colourful with pictures cut out of magazines. In the most conspicuous place, near the ikons, hung a portrait of Battenberg, once Prince of Bulgaria. Antip Sedelnikov stood by the table with his arms crossed.

'This one 'ere owes a hundred and nineteen roubles, your honour,' he said when it was Osip's turn. ''E paid a rouble before Easter, but not one kopek since.'

The inspector looked up at Osip and asked, 'How come, my dear friend?'

'Don't be too hard on me, your honour,' Osip said, getting very worked up, 'just please let me explain, sir. Last summer the squire from Lyutoretsk says to me, "Sell me your hay, Osip, sell it to me ..." Why not? I had about a ton and a half of it, what the women mowed in the meadows

. . . well, we agreed the price . . . It was all very nice and proper.'

He complained about the elder and kept turning towards the other peasants as though summoning them as witnesses. His face became red and sweaty and his eyes sharp and evil-looking.

'I don't see why you're telling me all this,' the inspector said. 'I'm asking *you* why you're so behind with your rates. It's *you* I'm asking. None of you pays up, so do you think *I'm* going to be responsible!'

'But I just can't!'

'These words have no *consequences*, your honour,' the elder said. 'In actual fact those Chikildeyevs belong to the *impecunious* class. But if it please your honour to ask the others, the whole reason for it is vodka. And they're real troublemakers. They've no *comprehension*.'

The inspector jotted something down and told Osip in a calm, even voice, as though asking for some water, 'Clear off!'

Shortly afterwards he drove away and he was coughing as he climbed into his carriage. From the way he stretched his long, thin back one could tell that Osip, the elder and the arrears at Zhukovo were no more than dim memories, and that he was now thinking about something that concerned him alone. Even before he was half a mile away, Antip Sedelnikov was carrying the samovar out of the Chikildeyevs' hut, pursued by Grannie, who was shrieking for all she was worth, 'I won't let you have it, *I won't*, blast you!'

Antip strode along quickly, while Grannie puffed and panted after him, nearly falling over and looking quite 77 ferocious with her hunched back. Her shawl had slipped down over her shoulders and her grey hair, tinged with green, streamed in the wind. Suddenly she stopped and began beating her breast like a real rebel and shouted in an even louder sing-song voice, just as though she were sobbing, 'Good Christians, you who believe in God! Heavens, we've been trampled on! Dear ones, we've been persecuted. Oh, please help us!'

'Come on, Grannie,' the elder said sternly, 'time you got some sense into that head of yours!'

Life became completely and utterly depressing without a samovar in the Chikildeyevs' hut. There was something humiliating, degrading in this deprivation, as though the hut itself were in disgrace. It wouldn't have been so bad if the elder had only taken the table, all the benches and pots instead – then the place wouldn't have looked so bare as it did now. Grannie yelled, Marya wept and the little girls looked at her and wept too. The old man felt guilty and sat in one corner, his head downcast and not saying a word. Nikolay did not say a word either: Grannie was very fond of him and felt sorry for him, but now all compassion was forgotten as she suddenly attacked him with a stream of reproaches and insults, shaking her fists right under his nose. He was to blame for everything, she screamed. And in actual fact, why had he sent them so little, when in his letters he had boasted that he was earning fifty roubles a month at the Slav Fair? And why did he have to come with his family? How would they pay for the funeral if he died . . .? Nikolay, Olga and

Sasha made a pathetic sight.

The old man wheezed, picked his cap up and went off to see the elder. Already it was getting dark. Antip Sedelnikov was soldering something near the stove, puffing his cheeks out. The air was heavy with fumes. His skinny, unwashed children – they were no better than the Chikildeyev children – were playing noisily on the floor, while his ugly, freckled, pot-bellied wife was winding silk. It was a wretched, miserable family – with the exception of Antip, who was handsome and dashing. Five samovars stood in a row on a bench. The old man offered a prayer to Battenberg and said, 'Antip, have pity on us, give us the samovar back, for Christ's sake!'

'Bring me three roubles – then you can have it back.'

'I haven't got them!'

Antip puffed his cheeks out, the fire hummed and hissed and its light gleamed on the samovars. The old man rumpled his cap, pondered for a moment and said, 'Give it back!'

The dark-faced elder looked jet-black, just like a sorcerer. He turned to Osip and said in a rapid, stern voice, 'It all depends on the magistrate. At the administrative meeting on the 26th inst. you can announce your grounds for dissatisfaction, orally or in writing.'

Osip did not understand one word of this, but he seemed satisfied and went home.

About ten days later the inspector turned up again, stayed for an hour and then left. About this time the weather was windy and cold. The river had frozen over long ago, but there still hadn't been any snow and everyone was miserable, as the roads were impassable. On one holiday, just before evening, some neighbours dropped in at Osip's for a chat.

The conversation took place in the dark – it was considered sinful to work, so the fire had not been lit. There was a little news – most of it unpleasant: some hens had been confiscated from two or three households that were in arrears and taken to the council offices where they died, since no one bothered to feed them. Sheep were confiscated as well – they were taken away with their legs tied up and dumped into a different cart at every village; one died. And now they were trying to decide who was to blame.

'The local council, who else?' Osip said.

'Yes, of course, it's the council.'

The council was blamed for everything – tax arrears, victimization, harassment, crop failures, although not one of them had any idea what the function of the council was. And all this went back to the times when rich peasants who owned factories, shops and inns had served as councillors, became dissatisfied, and cursed the council when they were back in their factories and inns. They discussed the fact that God hadn't sent them any snow: firewood had to be moved, but it was impossible to drive or walk because of all the bumps in the road. Fifteen or twenty years ago – or even earlier – the local gossip in Zhukovo was much more interesting. In those times every old man looked as though he was hiding some secret, knew something, and was waiting for something. They discussed deeds with golden seals, allotments and partition of land, hidden treasure and they were always hinting at something or other. But now the people of Zhukovo had no secrets at all: their entire lives were like an open book, which anyone could read and all they could talk about was

poverty, cattle feed, lack of snow . . .

They fell silent for a while: then they remembered the hens and the sheep and tried to decide whose fault it was.

'The council's!' Osip exclaimed gloomily. 'Who else!'

8

The parish church was about four miles away, at Kosogorovo, and the people only went there when they really had to – for christenings, weddings or funerals. For ordinary prayers they went to the church across the river. On saints' days (when the weather was fine) the young girls put on their Sunday best and crowded along to Mass, making a very cheerful picture as they walked across the meadows in their yellow and green dresses. But when the weather was bad everyone stayed at home. Pre-communion services were held in the parish church. The priest fined anyone who had not prepared for Communion during Lent fifteen kopeks as he went round the huts at Easter with his cross.

The old man didn't believe in God, for the simple reason that he rarely gave him a moment's thought. He admitted the existence of the supernatural, but thought that it could only affect women. Whenever anyone discussed religion or the supernatural with him, or questioned him, he would reluctantly reply as he scratched himself, 'Who the hell knows!'

The old woman believed in God, but only in some vague way. Everything in her mind had become mixed up and no sooner did she start meditating on sin, death and salvation, than poverty and everyday worries took charge and immediately she forgot what she had originally been thinking about. She could not remember her prayers and it was usually in the evenings, before she went to bed, that she stood in front of the ikons and whispered, 'to the Virgin of Kazan, to the Virgin of Smolensk, to the Virgin of the Three Arms . . .'

Marya and Fyokla would cross themselves and prepare to take the sacrament once a year, but they had no idea what it meant. They hadn't taught their children to pray, had told them nothing about God and never taught them moral principles: all they did was tell them not to eat forbidden food during fast days. In the other families it was almost the same story: hardly anyone believed in God or understood anything about religion. All the same, they loved the Bible dearly, with deep reverence; but they had no books, nor was there anyone to read or explain anything to them. They respected Olga for occasionally reading to them from the Gospels, and spoke to her and Sasha very politely.

Olga often went to festivals and services in the neighbouring villages and the county town, where there were two monasteries and twenty-seven churches. Since she was rather scatterbrained, she tended to forget all about her family when she went on these pilgrimages. Only on the journey home did she suddenly realize, to her great delight, that she had a husband and daughter, and then she would smile radiantly and say, 'God's been good to me!'

Everything that happened in the village disgusted and tormented her. On Elijah's day they drank, on the Feast of the Assumption they drank, on the day of the Exaltation of the Cross they drank. The Feast of the Intercession was a parish holiday in Zhukovo, and the men celebrated it by going on a three-day binge. They drank their way through fifty roubles of communal funds and on top of this they had a whip-round from all the farms for some vodka. On the first day of the Feast, the Chikildeyevs slaughtered a sheep and ate it for breakfast, lunch and dinner, consuming vast quantities, and then the children got up during the night for another bite. During the entire three days Kiryak was terribly drunk – he drank everything away, even his cap and boots, and he gave Marya such a thrashing that they had to douse her with cold water. Afterwards everyone felt ashamed and sick.

However, even in Zhukovo or 'Lackeyville', a truly religious ceremony was once celebrated. This was in August, when the ikon of the Life-giving Virgin was carried round the whole district, from one village to another. The day on which the villagers at Zhukovo expected it was calm and overcast. Right from the morning the girls, in their Sunday best, had left their homes to welcome the ikon and towards evening it was carried in procession into the village with the church choir singing and the bells in the church across the river ringing out loud. A vast crowd of villagers and visitors filled the street; there was noise, dust, and a terrible crush . . . The old man, Grannie, and Kiryak all held their hands out to the ikon, looked at it hungrily and cried out tearfully, 'Our Protector, holy Mother!'

It was as though everyone suddenly realized that there wasn't just a void between heaven and earth, that the rich and the strong had not grabbed everything yet, that there was still someone to protect them from slavery, crushing, unbearable poverty – and that infernal vodka.

'Our Protector, holy Mother!' Marya sobbed. 'Holy Mother!'

But the service was over now, the ikon was taken away and everything returned to normal. Once again those coarse drunken voices could be heard in the pub.

Only the rich peasants feared death, and the richer they became, the less they believed in God and salvation – if they happened to donate candles or celebrate Mass, it was only for fear of their departure from this world – and just to be on the safe side. The peasants who weren't so well off had no fear of death.

Grannie and the old man had been told to their faces that their lives were over, that it was time they were gone, and they did not care. They had no qualms in telling Fyokla, right in front of Nikolay, that when he died her husband Denis would be discharged from the army and sent home. Far from having any fear of death, Marya was only sorry that it was such a long time coming, and she was glad when any of her children died.

Death held no terrors for them, but they had an excessive fear of all kinds of illness. It only needed some trifle – a stomach upset or a slight chill – for the old woman to lie over the stove, wrap herself up and groan out loud, without stopping, 'I'm dy-ing!' Then the old man would dash off to fetch the priest and Grannie would receive the last sacrament and extreme unction. Colds, worms and tumours that began in the stomach and worked their way up to the heart were everyday topics. They were more afraid of catching cold than anything else, so that even in summer they wrapped themselves in thick clothes and stood by the stove warming themselves. Grannie loved medical treatment and frequently went to the hospital, telling them there that she was fifty-eight, and not seventy: she reasoned if the doctor knew her real age he would refuse to have her as a patient and would tell her it was time she died, rather than have hospital treatment. She usually left early in the morning for the hospital, taking two of the little girls with her, and she would return in the evening, cross and hungry, with drops for herself and ointment for the little girls. Once she took Nikolay with her; he took the drops for about two weeks afterwards and said they made him feel better.

Grannie knew all the doctors, nurses and quacks for twenty miles around and she did not like any of them. During the Feast of the Intercession, when the parish priest went round the huts with his cross, the lay-reader told her about an old man living near the town prison, who had once been a medical orderly in the army and who knew some very good cures. He advised her to go and consult him, which Grannie did. When the first snows came she drove off to town and brought a little old man back with her: he was a bearded, Jewish convert to Christianity who wore a long coat and whose face was completely covered with blue veins. Just at that time some jobbing tradesmen happened to be working in the hut – an old tailor with terrifying spectacles was cutting a waistcoat from some old rags and two young men were making felt boots from wool. Kiryak, who had been given the sack for drinking and lived at home now, was sitting next to the tailor mending a horse-collar. It was cramped, stuffy and evil-smelling in the hut. The convert examined Nikolay and said that he should be bled, without fail.

He applied the cupping glasses, while the old tailor, Kiryak and the little girls stood watching – they imagined that they could actually see the illness being drawn out of Nikolay. And Nikolay also watched the cup attached to his chest slowly filling with dark blood and he smiled with pleasure at the thought that something was really coming out.

'That's fine,' the tailor said. 'Let's hope it does the trick, with God's help.'

The convert applied twelve cups, then another twelve, drank some tea and left. Nikolay started shivering. His face took on a pinched look, like a clenched fist, as the women put it; his fingers turned blue. He wrapped himself tightly in a blanket and a sheepskin, but he only felt colder. By the time evening came he was very low. He asked to be laid on the floor and told the tailor to stop smoking. Then he fell silent under his sheepskin and passed away towards morning.

9

What a harsh winter it was and what a long one!

By Christmas their own grain had run out, so they had to buy flour. Kiryak, who was living at home now, made a dreadful racket in the evening, terrifying everyone, and in the mornings he was tormented by self-disgust and hangovers; he made a pathetic sight. Day and night a hungry cow filled the barn with its lowing, and this broke Grannie and Marya's hearts. And, as though on purpose, the frosts never relented in their severity and snowdrifts piled up high. The winter dragged on: a real blizzard raged at Annunciation and snow fell at Easter.

However, winter finally drew to an end. At the beginning of April it was warm during the day and frosty at night – and still winter hadn't surrendered. But one warm day did come along at last and it gained the upper hand. The streams flowed once more and the birds began to sing again. The entire meadow and the bushes near the river were submerged by the spring floods and between Zhukovo and the far side there was just one vast sheet of water with flocks of wild duck flying here and there. Every evening the fiery spring sunset and rich luxuriant clouds made an extraordinary, novel, incredible sight – such clouds and colours that you would hardly think possible seeing them later in a painting.

Cranes flashed past overhead calling plaintively, as though inviting someone to fly along with them. Olga stayed for a long while at the edge of the cliff watching the flood waters, the sun, the bright church which seemed to have taken on a new life, and tears poured down her face; a passionate longing to go somewhere far, far away, as far as the eyes could see, even to the very ends of the earth, made her gasp for breath. But they had already decided to send her back to Moscow as a chambermaid and Kiryak was going with her to work as a hall porter or at some job or other. Oh, if only they could go soon!

When everything had dried out and it was warm, they prepared for the journey. Olga and Sasha left at dawn, with rucksacks on their backs, and both of them wore bast shoes. Marya came out of the hut to see them off. Kiryak wasn't well and had to stay on in the hut for another week. Olga gazed at the church for the last time and thought about her husband. She did not cry, but her face broke out in wrinkles and became ugly, like an old woman's. During that winter she had grown thin, lost her good looks and gone a little grey. Already that pleasant appearance and agreeable smile had been replaced by a sad, submissive expression that betrayed the sorrow she had suffered and there was something blank and lifeless in her, as though she were deaf. She was sorry to leave the village and the people there. She remembered them carrying Nikolay's body and asking for prayers to be said at each hut, and how everyone wept and felt for her in her sorrow. During the summer and winter months there were hours and days when these people appeared to live worse than cattle, and life with them was really terrible. They were coarse, dishonest, filthy, drunk, always quarrelling and arguing amongst themselves, with no respect for one another and living in mutual fear and suspicion. Who maintains the pubs and makes the peasants drunk? The peasant. Who embezzles the village, school and parish funds and spends it all on drink? The peasant. Who robs his neighbour, sets fire to his house and perjures himself in court for a bottle of vodka? Who is the first to revile the peasant at district council and similar meetings? The peasant. Yes, it was terrible living with these people; nevertheless, they were still human beings, suffering and weeping like other people and there was nothing in their lives which did not provide some excuse: killing work which made bodies ache all over at night, harsh winters, poor harvests, overcrowding, without any help and nowhere to find it. The richer and stronger cannot help, since they themselves are coarse, dishonest and drunk, using the same foul language. The most insignificant little clerk or official treats peasants like tramps, even talking down to elders and churchwardens, as though this is their right. And after all, could one expect help or a good example from the mercenary, greedy, dissolute, lazy people who come to the village now and then just to insult, fleece and intimidate the peasants? Olga recalled how pathetic and down-trodden the old people had looked when Kiryak was taken away for a flogging that winter . . . and now she felt sorry for all these people and kept glancing back at the huts as she walked away.

Marya went with them for about two miles and then she made her farewell, prostrating herself and wailing out loud, 'Oh, I'm all alone again, a poor miserable wretch . . .'

For a long time she kept wailing, and for a long time afterwards Olga and Sasha could see her still kneeling there, bowing as though someone were next to her and clutching her head, while the rooks circled above.

The sun was high now and it was warm. Zhukovo lay far behind. It was very pleasant walking on a day like this. Olga and Sasha soon forgot both the village and Marya. They were in a gay mood and everything around was a source of interest. Perhaps it was an old burial mound, or a row of telegraph poles trailing away heaven knows where and disappearing over the horizon, with their wires humming mysteriously. Or they would catch a glimpse of a distant farm-house, deep in foliage, with the smell of dampness and hemp wafting towards them and it seemed that happy people must live there. Or they would see a horse's skeleton lying solitary and bleached in a field. Larks poured their song out untiringly, quails called to each other and the corncrake's cry was just as though someone was tugging at an old iron latch.

By noon Olga and Sasha reached a large village. In its broad street they met that little old man who had been General Zhukov's cook. He was feeling the heat and his sweaty red skull glinted in the sun. Olga and the cook did not recognize one another at first, but then they both turned round at once, realized who the other was and went their respective ways without a word. Olga stopped by the open windows of a hut which seemed newer and richer than the others, bowed and said in a loud, shrill sing-song voice, 'You good Christians, give us charity, for the sake of Christ, so that your kindness will bring the kingdom of heaven and lasting peace to your parents . . .'

'Good Christians,' Sasha chanted, 'give us charity for Christ's sake, so that your kindness, the kingdom of heaven . . .'